FIND YOU IN THE DARK

MARK GILLESPIE

Dedicated to
Richard 'Ricky' Stirling and
Robert McDonald

Go well.

PART I

BLACKMAIL

1

Laura opened her eyes. The ceiling that came into focus was all cracks and blemishes. Looked like puddles of splattered grease everywhere.

That wasn't *her* ceiling.

A whiff of stale smoke shot up her nostrils. Laura winced. Smoke? How many years had it been since she'd woken up to the odour of stale tobacco in the morning? Not since she was a teenager, at least. Back when she'd pretended to like smoking to fit in with the cool kids.

Something wasn't right.

Tommy didn't smoke. She didn't smoke. None of her friends smoked and hadn't done for at least ten years.

What have I done?

Whose bed is this?

Her sluggish mind seeped through hazy fragments of the night before. A highlight reel playing, a moving jigsaw puzzle with half the pieces missing. *Shit, shit, shit.* Friday night. She was in Bar 91 in Glasgow's Merchant City, celebrating Shauna's thirty-fourth birthday party. All the work people were there, the entire crew from Masons FX, a special effects and makeup company based in the west end. The Masons crew had taken over the pub and, by the end of the night, to call them rowdy would be the world's biggest understatement.

Laura didn't mean to get drunk. But when Becky, the young receptionist, danced her way back to the main table with the first tray of shots, it was game over for sobriety and rational thought. There'd been a big cheer. A lot of whooping and fist-pumping and people behaving badly.

The second tray of shots came soon after the first. Laura lost count after that.

There'd been a lot of women dancing on the tables. Laura might have been up there too, swayed by peer pressure. Swayed by the shots. More shots came after the second tray. Sweet-tasting poison. She'd even smoked a cigarette outside after asking some random guy if he had any spare. He'd tried to chat her up, thinking that the cigarette meant he was in there. Laura rebuffed his advances, flashing her engagement ring. He gave her a look that said, so what? She left him at the door, went back inside and drank and danced some more.

"Where am I?" she groaned.

Her head was drowning in a soft, spongy pillow. The mattress was a block of scalding granite, damp with night sweats. The heaviness she felt provoked a jolt of horror. Was she tied up? No, things were moving under the sheets. Her arms and legs, along with everything else, were just sluggish.

You're okay, she told herself.

"Good morning."

Laura sat up at the sound of the man's voice. At the same

time, the pain in her head went off like an explosion. There it was, the hangover from hell.

"Who's that?"

Her eyes skimmed the room. Floral lace curtains were closed over at the window, leaving everything in a gloomy haze. Laura strained her eyes. Saw a white rectangle fixed to the back of the door with 'Evacuation Plan' written at the top in bold letters. It was too dark to read anything else on the sheet. There was a welcome book on the desk. Hideous floral-patterned wallpaper and cheap furniture that belonged on the side of the street with a 'FREE' label stuck on the side. A musty smell emanated from the carpet. Smelled like something had died down there.

A hotel room? Laura had no memory of checking into a hotel.

"Good morning," the man repeated.

He was sitting in the corner, perched on the edge of a wooden chair. The window was to his left, partially open. A breeze came in, causing the lace curtains to shudder. The sound of traffic drifted up from the street.

The man's shirt was unbuttoned to the waist, exposing a soft belly and hairy chest.

Laura's blood ran cold.

No, she thought. *Please God, no.*

She was fully naked under the covers. As the man popped a cigarette into his mouth, Laura grabbed the sheets and pulled them all the way up to her neck.

God, she was covered in sweat.

The man lit up with a cheap Bic lighter. His inhale was a loud sucking hiss.

Laura didn't let go of the sheets. "Who are you? What am I doing here?"

"You don't remember?"

"No."

He smiled, as if she'd said something funny. Laura didn't understand. *What the fuck was she doing here?* Who was this guy? He was in his mid-to-late thirties, a plain-looking man. Dull eyes. Thin lips. Brown hair, short back and sides. Along with the unbuttoned black shirt, he wore cream-coloured tracksuit bottoms with a line of faded red trim down the side.

His ring and middle fingers were covered in yellow-brown tar stains.

"Who are you?"

She saw a pile of clothes, neatly folded up on the chair beside the desk. Her clothes from last night. Everything, underwear included.

"Why am I here?"

Laura's head felt like it was about to explode. Every word she spoke was like a hammer drill to the temples.

"My name's Dirk."

He spoke with an accent. German or Dutch, or something like that.

There was something familiar about him. Now that she'd heard his voice a few times. Had she met him last night in the pub? It definitely wasn't the guy she'd taken a cigarette from at the door.

Memories of last night. Staggering back into the pub after the cigarette. Literally staggering, like a pissed-up idiot. More shots. Bright lights, loud music and dancing. But Laura was still alert enough to call it a night before things got too messy. That would've been around eleven o'clock. Maybe. Looking at the state of her colleagues, she knew there'd be casualties. Let the singles have their fun. Laura wanted no part of it. She was engaged to be married and all she wanted to do was go back home to Tommy and their little dog. Drink a pint of cold water, watch TV, and let Tommy carry her to bed.

The hardcore party people were heading to a club on Sauchiehall Street. Laura declined multiple offers to join them. She told them she was heading home. There were others fleeing the carnage too. Some of them organising taxis and Ubers. Laura could've jumped in with them, shared the cost of the ride home. But she'd already ordered a Budz, a smaller ridesharing app that she liked to use because, according to what she'd been told, it paid the drivers a better wage.

She remembered hanging around outside the pub, waiting for her car to arrive. She might have been standing out there for ten minutes. Getting dirty looks from cigarette guy because she'd shrugged off his advances.

At some point, a car pulled up outside the pub. She couldn't remember the model. Couldn't even remember the colour. It was too dark. Foggy memories of the bouncer helping Laura into the backseat. God, had she been that drunk? She fell into the car, some of her friends laughing hysterically behind her. Bastards. She'd waved. Made sure the driver had the right address before setting off. He turned around. Smiled at her.

This guy. Dirk.

"It's you," she said. "You were supposed to drive me home. Where am I? What the fuck am I doing here?"

Dirk sat up straight in the chair, smoke billowing from the red tip of the cigarette. "Relax, okay? It's important that you relax before we do this."

Laura gripped the sheets tighter, holding them like a shield. "Before we do what?"

He kept going with the calm voice. And yet Laura could hear the trembling underneath. "First things first. You're not in any physical danger. I promise. Nothing like *that* is going to happen to you."

Laura stared at the man. Was he out of his mind?

"Did we...?"

The throbbing in her head intensified. She pressed her fingers against the temples, massaging in a circular motion.

"Did we do...?"

Dirk made another sucking hiss as he inhaled. Then, he exhaled slowly, leaning back into the chair, tilting it onto the back legs.

"Sex? You want to know if we had sex?"

She bit her lip. "Yes."

"No. You have my word."

"Your word?" Laura said. What was the word of a kidnapping sleazebag worth? She hadn't conducted a thorough examination of her body, but she didn't feel any obvious discomfort. No cuts, scrapes or bruises. Nothing out of the ordinary that would suggest he'd violated her. "Tell me why I'm here. I mean, how did I even get here?"

Dirk smiled, as if she'd said something funny. "How did you get here? You walked. That is to say, you walked as well as you could under the circumstances."

"Under the circumstances?"

"You were very drunk last night, Laura."

Laura looked down at the sweat-soaked sheets covering her breasts. Then, she glared at Dirk. "Who undressed me?"

Dirk took one last wheezy drag of the cigarette. He stubbed it out on the sole of his shoe, then dropped the butt into a glass tumbler. The tumbler was packed with discarded butts floating in cloudy water. With a sigh, he stood up off the chair, his joints cracking.

He walked towards the bed.

Laura shrank backwards, still clutching the sheets to her

chest. Her back was pinned against the headboard. There was only the wall behind her. Dirk was blocking the path towards the door.

There was nowhere to go.

He smiled again.

"I'm not a rapist, Laura."

She watched as Dirk knelt down beside the bed. He picked something up off the floor and when he straightened back up, she saw that he was carrying an iPad with a small crack in the screen. With another sigh, Dirk sat down on the edge of the bed, the odour of stale cigarette smoke emanating from his skin and clothes. There were massive dark circles under his eyes. Looked like he hadn't slept in a month.

"Don't come any closer," Laura said. "I'll scream. There have to be other people in this hotel. They'll hear me. I'll make sure of it."

"I'm *not* a rapist."

She sat upright on the bed, rigid and taut. Raised her voice like it was weapon.

"Then why didn't you take me home last night? You know? Do your fucking job, man. I don't understand why the hell I've just woken up in some shitty hotel room with some creep I don't know sitting across the room with his shirt open. Why did you bring me here? Why did you undress me if you didn't–?"

Dirk put the iPad on his lap.

"I'll show you."

"Just tell me."

"It'll make sense in a minute, Laura."

The way he kept saying her name. Like she was a child.

Dirk opened an app on the home screen. With a half-smile on his face, he turned the iPad around, holding it up so that Laura could see the screen.

"What is this?"

"Let me give you fair warning," he said, with a long-drawn out sigh. "This won't be easy for you to watch."

2

Dirk played a video clip. His face wore an unflinching neutral expression as he looked back and forth between the screen and Laura's face. He might as well have been washing the dishes.

"What's this?" Laura asked.

"Just watch it."

It was hard to make out anything at first. The lighting in the clip was atrocious. Looked like it had been filmed by a blind man inside a dark wardrobe. There was audio though, scratchy and poor-quality. It was the sound of heavy breathing.

Laura shook her head. "What is it? What am I supposed to be looking at here?"

"Keep watching."

All of a sudden, the image brightened. It was as if the filmmaker had remembered to switch a light on. There was an explosion of shrill, hysterical laughter. The laughter came out tinny and distorted, like it was coming through an old-school transistor radio. The sound crackled its way through the feeble speakers. The camera began to move slowly around the room. Laura's heart sank as she recognised the flowery wallpaper of the hotel room. The desk. The lace curtains.

Then, the camera panned away from the window, slowly making its way towards the queen-sized bed.

Laura put a hand over her mouth.

"Oh God, no."

She was lying on top of the sheets, naked. It was her. She was the woman laughing and she was still going hard as the camera approached the bed in slow motion. Laura felt sick to her stomach. What was she thinking? Why was she laughing? It was like watching someone else. Some poor drunken fool to be pitied.

"What the hell is this?"

Her voice was the one shaking now. And it wasn't subtle.

"I said, what the hell is this?"

Dirk didn't answer so she continued to watch the film, as painful as it was. There was no way she'd been that drunk. Had she? She'd never been *that* drunk in her life, even during the wild teenage phase at around sixteen, seventeen. She had no memory of what was unfolding on the screen.

"What's going on here?"

"Keep watching," Dirk said, his monotone voice like a cold finger down the spine. "We'll talk after. For now, don't interrupt."

He was looking at Laura now, as if bracing himself for a sudden attack. But Laura didn't have it in her. Sudden or otherwise. Even if she had a hammer in hand, she didn't have the energy to throw herself forward and club the bastard on the head until his brains spilled out all over the floor. Nice fantasy though. In reality, she felt broken. Her back pushed tighter against the headboard, testing the paper-thin walls of the sleazy, smoke-filled room. There was a tight, knotting sensation in her stomach. The urge to throw up all over the cardboard sheets.

"Just answer me, please. Why are you doing this to me? What do you want?"

His voice was stern.

"We're not finished yet, Laura. Keep watching."

She winced.

Stop saying my fucking name like you know me.

The camera turned around, revealing a shot of Dirk's head. He zoomed out a little, his naked body coming into frame. Naked, at least, from the waist up. Thankfully, Dirk stopped there and didn't reveal any more of himself. His smile was tight-lipped. Eyes, intense. Unblinking. Laura continued to giggle in the background, making sober Laura cringe as she was forced to listen.

Laura couldn't believe this was happening. It was like watching a doppelganger messing everything up on her behalf.

Still, she had to see it.

Dirk brought the camera closer to his face. His pale olive skin was mapped with crooked lines. Every awkward expression looked like an experiment gone wrong. He grinned as he lowered himself onto the bed beside Laura. The bed creaked like an old door. Laura reached over, touching his flimsy shoulders. Then, she caressed his cheek. She blinked. There was a flicker of confusion in her eyes.

"Tommy?"

Dirk laughed, as if to block out the other man's name. The laughter was clumsy and forced. Then, he was fixated on camera angles, adjusting both his and Laura's position over and over again. Moving things around on the bed to make the footage look as natural as possible.

Laura sat on the bed, sheets pulled high, watching in

silence. Her neck was rigid. The tendons taut against her skin.

"I've seen enough. Turn it off."

"Okay."

He pushed a button on the iPad. The hotel room fell silent.

"What do you think of our little movie?" he asked.

Laura didn't answer.

"I spent a lot of time working on this," he said. "Later on, I'll do the editing and when that's over, it'll look even more convincing."

"I'll call the police," Laura said.

"No, you won't. That would be a mistake."

"You fucking bastard."

Laura buried her face in the sheets. The material reeked of some faint chemical odour. Quickly, she pulled her face away. Why was he doing this? Money, it had to be money. He was going to blackmail Laura with the footage unless she gave him money. That's how these things worked, right? Had to be some sort of scam going around with these rideshare drivers. Find a drunk woman. Kidnap her. Create suitable blackmail footage and wait for the money to roll in.

Dirk stood up off the bed, tucking the iPad under his arm. He returned to the chair beside the window, sitting down and lighting up another cigarette. He exhaled loudly, using his hand to waft the smoke towards the window.

"You see, Laura? I'm not a rapist."

"How do I know that for sure?"

Dirk's eyes lit up. "Looks pretty convincing, doesn't it? Well, I guess that's the point. But I can assure you, it wasn't rape. I'm trying to create something that looks like a consensual sexual encounter between two adults. Even with the rough footage as it is, it's not too bad. Hmm? You're not exactly fighting me off, are you?"

"I'm drunk."

"Will your boyfriend accept that excuse?" Dirk asked, leaning forward in the chair. He didn't blink. "What about your employers? What are they going to say when they see the heavily-edited version? And your poor parents? Will they see rape or consent? You're laughing. You're the one pulling me towards you."

"They'll believe whatever I tell them."

"No. They'll believe their own eyes."

Laura stared at the man. "What the hell is wrong with you?"

"Don't be alarmed," Dirk said, flicking ash into the over-crowded tumbler. He missed, the ash landing on the window ledge. "Nothing happened. Still, we put on a good show. That's the main thing."

"So, you wanted to make it look like we had sex?"

"I had to."

"*Had* to? Are you kidding me?"

Dirk narrowed his eyes. "Kidding? No, I can assure you that I'm not kidding. That's the last thing on my mind."

Laura glanced at her clothes folded up on the chair. What would he do if she threw off the sheets, leapt out of bed, grabbed the clothes and ran for the door at full speed? Would he try and stop her? Could he? There wasn't much to the man in terms of bulk. Looked like a stiff breeze could knock Dirk off his feet. Didn't matter. The idea was irrelevant because he'd shown her the video footage. That was as good as a pair of handcuffs locked around Laura's wrists and ankle.

"How much do you want?"

"Hmmm?"

"C'mon, let's get it over with. How much money do you want to keep this footage to yourself and not show it to anyone? A grand? Two grand? You know what, fuck you. I'm not paying. Doesn't matter how much you ask for. I'll tell everyone what happened. I'll tell them you kidnapped me and–"

"Kidnapped you?" Dirk said. He wagged a finger back and forth. Looked like he was disciplining a wayward child. "No. I don't think you were kidnapped. You walked through the front door of this hotel all by yourself. You walked past reception, got into the lift and entered this room. All by your lonesome. I didn't even touch you and the security cameras in the hotel, inside and out, will back me up. No one forced you to come here, Laura. No one kidnapped you."

There it was. The cruel smile. "And then of course, there's the footage itself. The footage with you laughing. Touching me."

"Fuck you."

"You should be flattered."

"What?"

"I chose you because you're so pretty."

"You *chose* me?"

The intensity of Dirk's gaze was unsettling. Laura couldn't seem to catch him in the act of blinking. Fucking lizard man, that's what he was. "You're just what I need hanging off my arm. She'll be livid when she sees you standing beside me."

"She?"

Laura looked at him. Was he crazy? Was Dirk a raving madman? Yet, it didn't fit. He seemed too calculating in that moment.

In all of this.

She clung to the sheets as Dirk picked up the silver hip

flask on the window ledge. He unscrewed the lid, sipping something that made him wince. With his face flushed, he sat up straight, offering the flask to Laura.

"Want some?"

She didn't answer.

Dirk shrugged, then put the hip flask back on the window ledge. He drummed his fingers off the ledge, a sluggish beat, then glanced down towards the street. His blank expression gave nothing away.

"While you were sleeping," he said. "I took the liberty of going through your social media accounts. Facebook, Twitter, Instagram. Your email too."

He pointed at Laura's phone on the bedside table.

Laura shook her head. "How did you–?"

"Unlock it?"

"Yes."

"I used your finger."

"Of course you did."

"You were sleeping so deeply, you didn't even notice. And now, I know so much about you, Laura. I know that you're half-Scottish, half-Danish. You turned twenty-seven earlier this year. You're a professional makeup and effects artist, working in Masons. You share your work on Instagram and Facebook. It's good. You have talent. You have a lot of friends, you like reading books – novels, mostly. Music. Movies. You like a lot of things. Your life, Laura, it looks very nice from the outside."

Laura nodded. "So, why do you want to ruin it?"

"I don't want to ruin anything."

She exhaled and it came out with the force of a left jab. "Can we just get straight to it? How much money do you want?"

The way Dirk looked at her. The way he tilted his head.

She felt like a specimen in a jar. Something deformed that belonged in an exhibit.

"Well?" she asked, the irritation in her voice obvious. "How much?"

Dirk shrugged. He went back to looking out the window. "I took the liberty of making a couple of Facebook posts for you."

Laura almost let go of the sheets. "You did what?"

"Look at your Facebook."

Laura kept one hand on the bedsheets. With the other, she reached over to the bedside table, picking up the phone like it might be boobytrapped. There was a glass of water on the table next to the phone. Laura's throat was a scorched desert. Still, she didn't pick up the glass. She unlocked her iPhone, opening the Facebook app. A feeling of dread swept through her as she waited for the app to open. It felt like cold hands wrapped around her throat. Laura looked at her profile page. Saw two posts had been added overnight.

"What have you done?"

"Laura, don't be so naïve. It's the twenty-first century after all. If you don't put it online, it didn't happen."

He laughed, as if somehow that was funny.

Laura kept her eyes on her profile page. The first post went up five hours ago. Text only. The drunken, all-caps rambling of someone pissed out of their head.

"SHIT-FACED IN BAR 91!! SHOUT OUT TO THE MASONS CREW!!!"

The text had a ridiculously long tail of laughing emojis. Wine glasses. Pint glasses. Cocktails. Laura noticed, to her horror, that there'd been plenty of responses and comments from her friends.

"Shit."

She clicked open the comments.

Bit shouty, no? Not like you darling. But you deserve to let your hair down. Have a great night!

WTF? Are you seventeen again?

Lol! God help them. Sounds like Laura's well and truly pissed.

Laura couldn't read any more of them. She'd never posted anything in her life that made her sound like a teenager at her first party. *God*, she thought. *How embarrassing.* Yet, people thought it was her. She checked out the second post, published four hours ago according to the Facebook timeline. This time it was a video. Laura glared at Dirk, then hit play. There was an explosion of music, distorted through the phone speaker. Laura quickly turned the volume to a low setting. She was looking at the inside of Bar 91. Listening to the sound of women cheering and singing along with the music. Whooping. Screaming. What a racket. Laura remembered filming this video, but she didn't remember it being *that* loud at the time. This was after several rounds of shots. The Masons crew had taken over the pub. Laura passed the phone around to the other girls, letting everyone have a go at filming the action. A gallery of inebriated faces, including Laura's, grinned back at the camera.

She stopped the clip. There were comments, but Laura didn't look at them.

"I don't understand," she said. "I don't understand what's going on here. What do you want? If it's money, will you just tell me-"

"I don't want a penny from you," Dirk said.

Laura didn't like the way he said it. And she could tell that he meant it too. This, whatever this was, wasn't about money.

"Those are the first two uploads," Dirk said. "You've already seen part three. That's what I keep on my iPad.

That's what I'm going to publish next. And not just on Face-book, but everywhere. I'll make sure your boyfriend, excuse me, your *fiancée*, sees it. Your family will see it too. Your employer. Anyone who matters to you."

Laura's life and reputation were hanging by a thread. What did this psycho want, if not money? She knew nothing about him. And God, the hangover was killing her. She didn't have the strength to deal with this. At a hundred percent, Laura might have thrown off the sheets, run over to the table, grabbed the manual and beat it off the guy's skull. Why not? Dirk wasn't exactly the Rock. Give it a go. Knock him out. Get his phone, get his iPad. Pick up any USB sticks lying around. Take it all and run.

But she was in no shape to fight.

"I want to go home," she said.

It was pathetic, but it was all she could manage. And it was true.

Dirk blew a cloud of smoke across the room and it floated lazily towards the ceiling. For a moment, he was hypnotised by its billowing trail. "Don't you want to know why you're here first?"

"I've asked a thousand times already."

"Have you?"

"Yes."

He nodded.

"I want a favour, that's all."

Laura cast a wary eye at the man in the chair. "A favour?"

"That's it."

"What sort of favour?"

"All I need is your time. One afternoon of your life. Tomorrow, preferably."

Laura heard a car horn blaring down on the street. The sound of shrieking brakes, then a brief shouting match between two drivers who knew all the best swear words in Glasgow. It was all background noise as far as Laura was concerned.

"An afternoon?"

"Yes."

"Doing what?"

"Helping me."

"How exactly?"

Dirk grinned. "Trust me."

"Trust you? What the hell are you smoking right now?"

Dirk's face stiffened. He sucked on the cigarette, as if it was his last hit. Made that loud hissing noise, as if to spite Laura. "What choice do you have?"

Laura groaned. "A favour. That's it?"

"That's it. You'll do it?"

"Now, just wait a minute. Depends what it is."

There was a smirk on Dirk's face as he leaned forward in the chair. He reached for the hip flask. Took a sip of the foul-smelling beverage and grimaced as it went down.

"If Tommy sees the footage," he said, "it'll destroy him. You know that. He won't ever be able to trust a woman again. Your parents will be crushed. Could they ever forgive you, I wonder? Their daughter, the slut."

Laura felt a scalding sensation in her chest.

"Your face is in the video too."

"That's okay. Some simple editing will fix that. Trust me, Laura, you'll be the star of the show. I'll make sure of it."

Another clumsy laugh.

Laura looked at the glass of water beside the bed. Her throat ached and she was desperate to drink it. She glanced at her clothes on the chair. So neatly folded, like it mattered how they looked. Her eyes went to the door with the evacuation plan on the back. She imagined running into the corridor outside. The stairs. The exit. Fresh air. She wanted to wake up in her own bed and find that the smoke-filled hotel room and the man inside were a bad dream.

"The favour. What is it?"

Dirk's eyes lit up. "You'll do it?"

"What is it?"

Dirk cleared his throat. His eyes went to the floor and there was another grimace on his face, this time without taking a drink. That one gesture aged him by ten years. "About a m-m-month ago, maybe more, my wife left me for another m-m-man."

He looked at her, as if waiting for a reaction.

Laura said nothing.

"She lives with him now in *our* house," Dirk said. "It's like I never existed. He sleeps in my bed. Makes love to my wife. I think my children call him D-D-Dad."

Dirk shook his head.

"No, I can't accept that."

He grabbed the hip flask again. Drank until there was nothing left and then slammed it down on the window ledge beside all the puddles of ash.

"Disgusting," he said.

Laura sat in bed, watching him. Still gripping the sheets like her life depended on it. "Why did she leave you?"

He pointed to the bedside table. "Would you like a glass of water, Laura? There's one right there, sitting right next to you."

She shook her head.

"Why did your wife leave you?"

She saw a violent twitch flaring up at the side of his eye. "I want Court, that's my wife, to feel the way that I feel when I see her with her b-b-beautiful Amir. I want that feeling to hit like a fist to her face."

"Amir?"

"Oh Amir, you should see him. Looks like one of those Bollywood heart throbs – tall, dark and handsome. Her Pakistani prince, ha. She's done well for herself. He's younger than me, fitter than me, and he's got a better job. Amir is the dashing knight who swept her off her feet at just the right time."

The violent twitch was spreading to his neck.

"W-w-why didn't she fight for our marriage? She made things hard for the children and yet she's the one who gets to keep them. How is that fair?"

Laura remained silent.

"It's just a fling," Dirk said, looking at his feet again. He paused, as if considering his words more carefully. "Court thinks it's love, but it's a bit of fun. It's a distraction. He'll soon get bored of her."

Laura's head felt like a pressure cooker about to explode. She didn't think she could take much more of Dirk's endless rambling about his marriage. On top of that, the reek of stale smoke inside the hotel room was killing her.

"What do you want me to do?"

Dirk ignored Laura's question. He continued talking to the floor. "I'm a fair man. I'm willing to forgive this indiscretion. For the sake of our c-c-children, you know? We were so young when we got together. *Too* young. It's a mistake, that's all. It's a mistake."

"Dirk," Laura said in a firm voice. "What's the favour?"

He growled. "*Need*. Not want. I need you to do it."

"Okay," Laura said, trying to breathe without taking in any more of that smoke. "What do you need me to do?"

His fingers slowly curled into a fist. As he tightened the balled fist, his arm shook all the way up to the shoulder.

"A woman."

"What?"

"I need a beautiful woman on my arm."

"What for?"

"She needs a shock to the system," Dirk said. "That should do it. That should remind her how much she needs me."

He was back talking to his feet.

"I know my wife. She thinks I haven't got a ch-ch-chance with anyone else and that I'll always be pining for her. Ha! She likes that. Makes her feel strong. In control. What better way to jolt her by showing her that other women find me desirable? And, not just any woman, but someone far better looking than she is."

He laughed. Kept his eyes on his feet. At this point, it didn't seem like he was talking to Laura. Just himself.

"See how she likes it."

Laura rubbed a hand over her aching temples. "Okay. This is messed up. You know that? This is really messed up."

So that was it? That was the reason that the Budz driver had kidnapped her. It wasn't about money. Wasn't about sex. It was all about childish mind games. About somebody else's failing marriage.

"This has nothing to do with me," Laura said.

"It does now."

"Does it?"

"You're here, aren't you?"

"Let me get this straight, *Dirk*. You kidnapped me because you want me to pretend to be your girlfriend?"

Dirk smiled, but it was a bitter smile. "Look at me, Laura. I'm just a poor Budz driver. I ferry entitled and obnoxious people around this horrible city. Day and night. I deliver food for extra money and sometimes they don't even look at me when they take the bag out of my hand. Let alone leave a tip. I'm invisible in this world. I take their shit because I have to. You think I can just go to a bar and pick up any woman I like?"

He glanced out of the window. Both hands still balled into tight fists.

"They're *my* family."

He pushed the flimsy curtains aside. The light that invaded the room turned Dirk's face milky, translucent white. He looked like a ghost.

"I just want them back. That's not too much to ask, is it? But no one will help me if I just ask. Not that I have anyone to ask. That's why you're here, Laura. I need you."

He pulled the curtains over again, as if the light was too much.

"Will you do it?"

"No," Laura said. She shook her head. "Have you thought about what you're doing here? This whole thing, it's ridiculous. I mean, it's *ridiculous*. I'm not going to pretend to be your girlfriend for a day. I don't know you and even if I did–"

Laura took a breath, trying to control the anger building up inside her. Letting it all out would have been glorious, but stupid.

"You know what? Go for it. Post your sleazy footage. I'll take it on the chin, tell them the truth. That you, the Budz driver, kidnapped me. I'll tell them everything and after that, you can wait for the police to come knocking on your door."

Dirk's mannequin-like expression didn't change.

"How many people saw you stagger out of Bar 91 last night? Watching you falling over as you tried to get in my car. Your hands all over the bouncer as he held you up. Your hands were all over me too after I got out to help. The bouncer, he saw the state you were in. All those people, they saw it. You were ready for anything."

Laura let out a quiet sigh. "And you saw your opportunity, didn't you?"

Dirk's cold stare was all the answer she needed.

"Is this the first time you've tried to kidnap a woman?" Laura asked. "Or have there been others before me?"

"People do stupid things when they're drunk," Dirk said, ignoring the question. "Are you willing to risk everything, Laura? You've seen the footage. You're laughing in it. Having the time of your life with a man you met on the way home. You're a willing participant, no matter what you say. Now, we're wasting time. Are you going to do it or not?"

"Fuck you."

"There's something else," he said. "Something you should know before making a decision. You were more than just drunk last night."

"What do you mean?"

"Think back, if you can. You were in my car. We're driving away from the pub. Do you remember that bottle of water? The one I offered you?"

Laura felt like she was drowning in the sweat-soaked mattress. The fabric clung to her skin, pulling her down as it cooled further. She closed her eyes, went back to last night. Tried to remember more of what happened after she left the pub. After she'd tumbled into Dirk's car. She recalled the bouncer's bald head poking through a gap in the back window, instructing the driver to take her straight home. And then? They were cruising through the city at night. Laura was talking to the driver. Small talk. He'd laughed and joked with her. Looking back, it all seemed a bit too forced. He asked if she was okay. Several times. Laura said something about going home and drinking a pint of water with ice in it. He laughed at that too. That clumsy, awkward laugh that was too forced. He'd reached a hand over the back, offering Laura a bottle of water. *Drink it up*, he'd said. *The sooner you start kicking that hangover's ass the better.* Or words to that effect.

They'd both laughed.

Laura didn't think twice. She'd been stupid. She'd been drunk. She took the bottle, fumbled with the lid and emptied it. After that, everything was a blur. She'd woken up in the hotel room, trapped in a nightmare.

"You bastard. What was in the bottle?"

Dirk shrugged. "Simple trade. Help me and no one ever sees the footage. Don't help me and you'll see if I'm bluffing."

Laura knew one thing for sure. The psycho wasn't bluffing. Not after everything he'd gone through to make this happen. She was cornered and they both knew it.

"This is so fucked up."

"Will you do it?" Dirk asked. "I'm running out of patience with you. One day, that's all I need from you. Court's waiting for me to collect the last of my things from the house. I've been putting it off for ages. How about Sunday?"

"Tomorrow?"

"Yes."

Laura pointed to her clothes on the chair. "If I say yes, can I go?"

"You're not a prisoner. You can go whenever you want."

Laura rolled her eyes. Maybe there weren't any steel bars keeping her in, but she *was* a prisoner. They both knew it.

"You'll do it."

She nodded.

"Say it."

"I'll do it."

"I've taken precautions," Dirk said, getting to his feet. His joints clicked as he walked towards the bed. "You should know this. You should believe it. Call it an insurance policy. If you try to back out, if you do anything foolish like go to the police, my insurance policy will trigger. Immediately. You understand? Our little pornographic movie will be all over the internet within twenty-four hours. I swear it on my children's life."

Laura gave a weak nod. "I understand. Will you turn around please? I'd like to put my clothes on and leave."

Dirk watched her for a moment. Then, he turned around so that he was facing the wall. He tilted his head back, as if looking up at all the stains in the ceiling.

"Take your clothes into the bathroom. You can get changed in there."

Laura's hands shook as she pushed the sheets back. She was suddenly cold, her skin soaked with sweat. She jumped out of bed, naked and sticky. Hurried over to the chair, grabbed her clothes, and rushed to the bathroom. On her way, she noticed that Dirk was mumbling to himself. Still staring up at the ceiling.

"A beautiful woman," he said, over and over again. "A beautiful woman to make her love me."

3

"Bit quiet tonight," Tommy said, putting an arm around Laura's shoulders. "Hangover that bad, is it?"

Laura kept her eyes on the TV. When Tommy squeezed her shoulder, she managed a weak nod of the head.

"Hmmm."

"Seriously. You're as white as a sheet."

Tommy giggled. That was the unspoken rule between them. No sympathy when the damage was self-inflicted. Tommy had had his fair share of hangovers throughout the years and Laura hadn't been shy of a joke or two at his expense.

Now it was her turn.

Except, it wasn't the hangover that troubled Laura. Not really. But she couldn't tell Tommy what it was making her sick to the stomach.

They were having a quiet night in their luxurious, three-bedroom Hyndland flat. It was a trendy spot, located in the west end of Glasgow. Nice cafes. Bistros. Wine bars. Having cancelled their plans to go out, Laura and Tommy were both flopped on the couch, watching a true crime documentary on TV.

"Shame we missed dinner tonight," Tommy said.

Laura was still looking at the TV. Not following any of it.

"We'll reschedule, okay? I'm sorry."

He shrugged. "I wasn't that fussed. Having said that, you get good grub there, eh? Last time we went I got the–"

"Please shut up about food."

"Sorry."

Laura *was* sorry about the missed dinner. They'd made plans to go out with their oldest friends, Robert and Jo. It'd been ages since they'd all been out together, just the four of them. Jo had given birth to their son, Teddy, ten months ago and ever since, there'd been less time for socialising without kids. They'd been planning to do something for ages. Finally, they'd settled upon a new Japanese restaurant, suggested by Robert. Laura had been looking forward to seeing their friends all week, not thinking for one moment that her Friday night antics would derail their plans. But the thought of eating was torture. She'd be lucky to make it into an Uber without puking or collapsing. Then she'd have to make conversation when all she could think about was what she'd seen on that creep's iPad.

About tomorrow.

What she had to do.

She'd told Tommy to go out with Robert and Jo anyway. No point in everyone missing out because Laura was suffering. Tommy said no. He insisted on staying home with her. And despite the 'no sympathy rule', he'd played the good fiancée, bringing her water and a wet dishtowel to keep her forehead cool. Laura was touched, but deep down she wanted Tommy to go out. She needed space to think. Now she had to sit there, interacting with another person, a

Herculean task, even if it was her soulmate sitting beside her. All she wanted to do was curl up in a ball and sleep, but she felt obliged to spend time with Tommy, especially as he'd given up Robert, Jo, and the Japanese restaurant for her.

"That's nasty," Tommy said, watching an incarcerated serial killer on TV talking about how he selected his female victims. The guy looked like a geography teacher. Spoke with a soft, almost girlish voice. "What's wrong with this guy? Drugging them and taking them back to his apartment? What a psycho. Glad I don't have a daughter."

Laura leaned her head against his shoulder. They'd been together for six years, engaged for one. In so many ways, they were chalk and cheese, especially when it came to work. Laura was the artist. Tommy was the suit – the left-brained, logical half. And yet, they were perfect together. One soul in two bodies. Their Hyndland flat was their pride and joy, decorated by Laura with very little input by Tommy, who was happy to let the professional artist do whatever she wanted.

Of course, he'd loved it.

This is a good life, she thought. *Better than good.*

Tonight, it was hanging by a thread. Laura had showered after coming home, but no matter how hard she scrubbed, she couldn't wash off the memory of what happened in the hotel room. She could smell smoke on her skin. On her fingers. Dirk's smoke.

Dirk.

The favour.

Fuck.

Just the thought of it made her feel queasy. Laura lifted her head off Tommy's shoulder and picked up the pint glass off the table. God, she wanted to drown herself in it. She poured the water down her throat, not stopping until the glass was empty. Then she put it back. Wiped her mouth dry and fell back onto the couch, feeling like a sponge that had been squeezed dry by merciless hands.

She couldn't think straight. She was still in that hotel room, still holding on to those sheets and inhaling the creep's smoke.

Laura had taken the bus home from the city centre. She couldn't bring herself to get in a taxi or an Uber.

Tomorrow.

She was scheduled to meet him tomorrow.

Did she really have to do this?

The footage. It was all about Dirk's sleazy little home movie. How could she doubt that her family and friends, people she'd known all her life, would stand by her if he leaked the footage? And yet she did. That's how bad it was. That's how bad it was *before* editing.

The man was unhinged. And he had her over a barrel.

Laura had checked herself upon coming home. There was no physical pain. No cuts, scrapes or bruises. No sexual encounter had taken place in the hotel room, she was willing to accept that. Not because she wanted to. She believed it. This was a psychological violation. He was fixated on winning his family back and Laura was a tool to be used.

She'd thought about telling Tommy. About going to the police. More times than she could count, but it all came back to the same thing.

The footage.

Laura couldn't do it.

All she had to do was pretend to be his girlfriend for a day. Then it would be over. Not even a full day. An afternoon. Maybe an hour or two.

She glanced at Tommy. He was looking at his phone, distracted by Twitter, scrolling through the feed like it was an Olympic sport. Like he was trying to get his thumb jacked. His legs were outstretched on the coffee table. Dressed in Adidas slacks, his black hair damp after a shower. There was a day's growth of stubble on his face, an unusual look for the well-groomed accountant.

Laura couldn't envision her life without this man. She'd imagined the look of shock on Tommy's face a hundred times already. Logging into his email account, clicking the link that would lead him to Dirk's footage.

He couldn't handle that. Even if he did believe her. Seeing her like that, it would break him.

It would break *them*.

"You alright sweetheart?" he asked, rubbing her back gently. "Don't think I've ever seen you this bad before."

Laura's voice was hoarse. "I'm fine."

Tommy smiled and went back to his phone. He was on Facebook now. Looking at Laura's posts from last night. He played the video that featured a horde of drunken women dancing on the tables in Bar 91. Laura squirmed beside him, wishing he'd turn it off. Tommy laughed, as if it was all a big joke. Never in a million years would Laura have posted anything like that. Her parents were on Facebook for God's sake. She should've deleted the clip, but so many people had seen it already. They'd reacted. They'd commented. What was the point of taking it down now?

Besides, how would Dirk react if she took it down?

Tommy leaned back on the couch. Still laughing to himself. "Looks like a fun night was had by all."

"Can you please turn that off?" Laura said, trying to grab the phone off Tommy. He dodged the attempt with ease.

"You're such a child. I thought we were supposed to be watching this serial killer thing."

Tommy glanced at the TV. "Next episode. It's about stalkers now."

"Whatever."

"How pissed were you last night?" Tommy said, his attention back on Laura's Facebook timeline.

She scowled. "The video says it all."

Tommy nodded. "Nice of Allie to let you stay at her flat last night, eh?"

Laura squirmed. Allie's flat. That was the official story she'd given Tommy. The story she'd come up with on the bus ride home. That was the reason she didn't come home last night. She told him she'd passed out in the pub and that Allie had insisted on looking after her. They'd taken an Uber together. Laura spent the night on Allie's couch, end of story. Thank God, Tommy believed her. He had no reason to think she'd lie about it. They didn't lie to each other, ever. Still, she'd have to say something down the line to Allie. Just in case Tommy ever brought it up.

Tommy put the phone down on the armrest. He looked at the TV, then at Laura. "It's nice to see you letting your hair down. You work too hard."

Laura managed a flimsy smile. She'd have to go to bed soon. There was no way she could sit up and make small talk for much longer.

"I have to go out for a couple of hours tomorrow afternoon."

She said it like it was no big thing.

Tommy scooped his wine glass off the table. He looked at his fiancée, then took a sip. "Sure you'll be up for it?"

"Yep."

"Back to the pub, is it?"

"Very funny. I'm going to the cinema with Sandy."

"Who?"

"Sandy, one of the new interns."

"Right."

"I told you that she's been lonely since moving back here from Australia."

Tommy frowned. "Did you?"

"You clearly weren't listening."

"Sorry."

"Anyway, I don't think she's quite got back into the swing of things at home or at work. It'll be good for her to get out of the house. She probably wants to get some things off her chest about the move and stuff. You know? Things she can't say at work."

"Fair enough."

Laura dragged up another smile. "We weren't planning on doing anything together, were we?"

Tommy shook his head, then stifled a yawn.

"Nah, I'll take Freddie for a walk down to the Botanics tomorrow. You know how much he loves sniffing around down there. I'll stretch my legs. That's about as adventurous as I feel like getting until Monday morning."

"Sounds good."

"What time you heading out?" Tommy asked.

"Umm, no later than eleven."

"Cool."

They didn't talk much after that. Tommy watched TV while Laura closed her eyes, the narrator's voice slipping off into the background. She didn't want to hear about stalkers. She had her own monster to deal with. Still, Laura couldn't drift off to a peaceful sleep, not even with her head on Tommy's shoulder.

She could see that sick bastard.

He was living in her head. That hiss-like suck on the cigarette. Loud sipping from the hip flask. His skeletal grin on full display, making Laura's blood run cold.

Just do what he wants, Laura thought. *It'll all be over by this time tomorrow.*

4

Laura woke up a little after nine o'clock on Sunday morning.

She lay in bed for a while, taking stock of her condition. Staring up at the ceiling. The hangover was gone, thank God. She wasn't operating at a hundred percent and there was still a faint gnawing sensation at her temples. But, compared to yesterday, she was in better shape.

She threw back the sheets. Her legs shivered in the cold as she set them down on the wooden floor. Laura tiptoed out of the bedroom, trying not to wake up Tommy and Freddie, their West Highland Terrier. Both man and dog were fast asleep on the bed. Both snoring the roof off the place. Tommy had stayed up late, watching a run of Marvel movies on Disney Plus and eating Domino's pizza while Laura had crashed early with another pint of water beside her on the bedside table.

She'd slept like a log.

I'm never drinking again, she thought, walking to the bathroom.

She took a hot shower, dried her hair and tried to figure

out what to wear for the role of Dirk's pretend girlfriend. What was she was supposed to go for? Dirk's instructions, which had come via text, were vague. Smart casual. Not too forced. He didn't want to arouse Court's suspicions about his new girlfriend.

Another text from Dirk came through while Laura was in the bathroom.

Don't look like a model. But don't look like a slut either. Just look nice.

"Fuck you."

Laura deleted the text. She went to the spare room where she kept most of her clothes. She opened up the massive wardrobe and picked out a long sleeve top and dark jeans. The sweater and jeans combo showed off her figure, but not in an obvious way. Not in a *slutty* way. Black slip-on shoes. A subtle layer of makeup.

She stood in front of the full-length mirror.

It was good enough. Nothing she could do about the panic in her eyes though.

She walked into the bedroom, leaned over the bed and kissed Tommy on the forehead. He rolled over onto his back, grunting something that Laura didn't understand. Freddie was a scruffy white ball curled up on Laura's pillow. Laura gave him a rub on the back. Freddie opened his eyes, gave her fingers a quick lick before going back to sleep.

"See you later boys," Laura whispered.

She left the flat, making a mental note to check out what films were showing today in town. She'd have to give Tommy a title when she came back. With any luck, there'd be a rom-com out. Tommy wouldn't ask questions about a rom-com.

Twenty-minutes later, she was on Great Western Road. It was already getting busy with walkers and shoppers as

Dirk's Toyota Corolla pulled up at the kerb beside her. Dirk rolled down the passenger side window. As the engine hummed, he looked Laura over, his face strained in concentration. He studied her clothes. Her face. Everything. Eventually, he gave her a nod of approval.

"Get in."

Laura reached for the door handle. She paused. What the hell was she doing? Getting in a car with this man. Was she crazy?

"Get in," Dirk said. The impatience was clear in his voice.

Laura pulled the door open and sunk down into the passenger seat. Her nostrils flinched. Stale smoke, there it was again. The smell of rubber. And something that reminded Laura of stale cat urine.

Run, said the voice in her head. *Open the door and run.*

They didn't talk as Dirk pulled away from the kerb. Laura fumbled with the seatbelt. She finally locked the tongue into the buckle. Eyes down, looking at the footrest. She was afraid that someone on the street would recognise her.

"Is it far?" she asked.

"Not far."

She glanced at Dirk. Looked like he'd made an effort. He was dressed in a pale blue shirt and dark jeans. His brown hair, slick with gel and combed into a side parting. He was clean shaven. The man looked nothing like the wretch she'd woken up to in the hotel room yesterday morning.

Dirk took the Corolla east on Great Western Road. A right turn onto the fashionable Byres Road. Laura kept looking at the floor. There were too many people out. Shopping. Meeting for breakfast, like they did every other Sunday. Afterwards, some of them would be heading to the bars and restaurants of Ashton Lane for a pub lunch and a few drinks. Laura knew a lot of these people. They'd know her at a glance. What would they think if they saw her in Dirk's car? What conclusions would they leap to?

"You're quiet," Dirk said. "Is something wrong?"

She raised her eyebrows.

"Are you serious?"

A long pause.

"What did you tell your boyfriend?"

Laura sighed. "I told my *fiancé* that I was going to the cinema with a friend."

"That's good. That means we've got plenty of time."

"Plenty of time?" Laura said, eyeing the pedestrians warily. "How much time do you need? This is straightforward, right? It's a one-off. I go with you to your wife's house today and whatever happens after that, it's got nothing to do with me. Okay?"

Sounded like she was making demands. Dirk held all the cards, but there was no way this messed up situation was anything but a one-off.

This is a mistake, she thought. *This is a big mistake.*

Dirk wasn't in much of a talking mood. That was okay with Laura. He stopped at a set of traffic lights where Byres Road merged with Dumbarton Road. He pushed the indicators, signalling a right turn. Looked like they were heading towards Partick.

He drove west, going straight through at a large roundabout that took them into Whiteinch. Not the nicest part of Glasgow. Laura didn't know anyone here. She was able to look outside at least without the fear of being recognised. An old man in a raincoat and beanie hat walked past on the pavement, dragging a shopping cart behind him. There were the usual pasty-faced teenagers in tracksuits and caps, walking with exaggerated monkey swagger, trying to impress and intimidate.

"Nearly there," Dirk said.

He gripped the steering wheel tight. Like he was about to yank it off.

The Corolla slowed as it passed the old primary school on Medwyn Street. The school was on one side of the street, a block of blonde and red sandstone flats on the other. The top half of Medwyn Street was newer. A collection of semi-detached houses.

That's where they were going.

The car pulled up outside a house at the end of the street. Number thirty-six. Laura looked at the exterior, her heart thumping in her chest. Black metal gate. Small driveway. There was a silver Fiesta parked out front.

It was a modest-looking dwelling. Modest, but comfortable.

Dirk pulled the handbrake. He turned off the engine, which prompted an uncomfortable silence inside the car.

After a minute, he looked at Laura. Eyes moist with tears.

"Help me. Please. I know what you must think of me, but I'm a n-n-nice person. I swear. I'm desperate."

The twitch flared up at the side of his eye. The one Laura had noticed in the hotel room yesterday.

"I just want my family back."

Laura arched her eyebrows. "How do I know you'll keep your end of the bargain?"

Dirk slapped the steering wheel in frustration. His voice was an angry hiss. "Why are you making this about you? I explained yesterday, didn't I? Make her jealous. I won't bother you ever again."

"You want me to help you? How can I be sure you won't

come creeping back into my life down the line, looking for more favours? How do I know that disgusting footage will be erased forever?

He slammed his back against the driver's seat. Breathing hard. Looking at the house. Looking at Laura.

"I'll do it. I've got no reason to keep it."

Laura wasn't convinced, but what choice did she have? She looked at the house again. Still no sign of life in number thirty-six. It was the weekend. What if nobody was home? That wasn't a pleasant thought. Laura wanted this thing done and dusted today. It had to end. That meant, assuming that Dirk's wife was in the house, that she had to get in character. She had to sell the pretty-girlfriend-besotted-with-Dirk act.

Get me out of here.

"You look nice," Dirk said. He attempted a smile. It backfired and made his face look like a Halloween mask.

"Thanks."

"We can do this," he said. "But it has to be convincing. I'll have to kiss you, okay? And when I do, you kiss me back and make it look good. Make it look authentic. If she doesn't believe us, you know what happens."

His weak smile fizzled out.

"You're talking about a peck on the cheek, right?" Laura asked. "That's all?"

"Of course. I'm not going to jump your bones in front of my wife and children."

Laura nodded. "I'll do my best."

"Do better."

Dirk took several deep breaths. Then, he pushed the handle down and nudged the car door open with his shoulder. Laura heard the psycho mumbling to himself as he stepped outside onto the pavement. She couldn't make out what he was saying. Sounded like some motivational bull-shit that he'd scraped off the internet.

The front door of the house creaked open as Dirk stepped out of the car. Laura looked over and saw a man standing in the doorway. Tall, dark-skinned. There was a troubled expression on his face. It had to be Amir. Not exactly the Bollywood hunk that Dirk had told Laura about. Still, he was easier on the eye than Dirk. He was in his early to mid-thirties. Casually dressed in a maroon t-shirt and jeans. Looked like his quiet Sunday at home had just been interrupted for the worse.

Dirk was a statue beside the car. Frozen in a rigid pose, fists clenched at the sides. The two men glared at one another over the fence.

"C'mon," Dirk said.

He was talking to Laura.

Now it was her turn to take a deep breath. She opened the door. Stepped outside. Straightened up and turned towards the house. Laura looked at Dirk and when she saw his face, she felt a cold chill shooting up her spine.

Dirk's eyes were watering. His bottom lip trembled. When he finally spoke, it felt like he was wrenching a tightly-clenched jaw loose.

"You see him? Do you see him?"

Laura nodded. "Yes."

"That's the bastard who stole my children."

5

Laura followed Dirk towards the gate. Chin up. Forcing a smile onto her face, trying to look like someone who wanted to be there.

Sell it, she reminded herself. *Sell the lie. Remember what's at stake.*

The enormity of the task hit like a punch in the face.

Dirk stopped like a vampire who'd got his first whiff of garlic. His eyes were dead now, no sign of the emotion that had leaked in the car moments earlier. He placed both hands on top of the metal gate.

Amir was still framed in the doorway, his body blocking the entrance to the house.

"Can I help you, Dirk?"

Laura felt her skin crawl. Something in Amir's eyes, in his alert, upright posture, suggested that previous encounters between them had been hostile. Threats? Perhaps violence. The tension was palpable.

Dirk's voice was a gruff bark. "I've come for my things."

"Have you?"

"I'm here, aren't I? Isn't this what you both wanted?"

Laura stood behind Dirk, squirming. Trying to hold onto a slippery smile that must have looked as fake as it felt. She felt a stab of resentment, stuck here in the thick of someone else's domestic hell. Tossed into the fire by a jilted psycho who wouldn't accept that his marriage was over.

Just do what he asks, Laura reminded herself. *It'll soon be over.*

And always the lingering doubt.

How can I trust him?

Dirk and Amir remained still, at the gate and front door respectively, engaged in a staring contest. Amir glanced at Laura. A flicker of confusion in his eyes. Doubt. Then, his attention turned back to Dirk.

"You want your things?"

Dirk nodded. "I said so, didn't I?"

"Took you long enough. The boxes have been sitting in the shed for months. Taking up room."

"I hope they didn't get wet."

"Quite frankly, I don't care if they did. If you were so concerned about your belongings, Dirk, you would've picked them up sooner."

Laura could see the veins sticking out on Dirk's neck. With every syllable Amir spoke, the man's jugular swelled to the point where Dirk began to look like a special effects prop from a horror movie. Before he could respond to Amir, a woman appeared in the doorway. Mid-thirties, slim and pale-skinned. Peroxide blonde hair, tied back into a pony-tail. She squeezed past Amir and walked down the doorstep. As she felt the cold, she pulled the ends of her cream-coloured cardigan together.

The wariness in Court's eyes was unmistakable.

"What are you doing here?"

"My things. I've come for them."

Dirk stepped to the left, a subtle move, one that allowed Court a clear view of Laura. Then, he began to unlatch the gate, working the bolt. Eyes never leaving Court. He pushed the gate open and it squeaked in a way that would have been comical in any other situation.

"Are the boxes still in the shed?" Dirk asked, walking up the garden path. He stopped. Bloodshot eyes burning. "You haven't thrown them away?"

Court glanced at Laura. Her cheeks glowed bright red.

"No, I haven't thrown them away. But I should have. It's taken you long enough to get around to picking them up. What have you been doing?"

"Been busy," Dirk said.

Laura was certain (as Court most likely was too) that the delay was a deliberate move on Dirk's part. A tactical manoeuvre to save his marriage. The longer he put it off, the more chance he had of weaselling his way back into the house. No boxes, no reminder of the man, the husband, or the father.

Which meant this was last chance saloon for Dirk. If he didn't get the reaction he wanted from Court, his marriage was over.

"Hello," Court said to Laura.

Laura was taken by surprise. She waved. It was too much and her arm flopped back to the side. She was the one blushing now. Bad start.

"Hi. It's nice to meet you."

Court looked at Dirk, waiting for an introduction.

Laura felt Dirk's fingers glide along the small of her back. She flinched. Might as well have been a poisonous snake wrapping itself around her body. She let out a spurt of nervous laughter as Dirk pulled her closer.

Who was she kidding?

"This is Laura," Dirk said. His voice boomed, as if he was introducing her to everyone on the street. "She's my girlfriend."

Court didn't blink.

"Wow. And how long have you lovebirds been together?"

Dirk nudged Laura with his elbow. Lips fumbling, trying to remember the shape of a smile. "Ooh, how long's it been sweetheart? A couple of weeks now?"

Laura froze. Everyone was looking at her. Waiting for her to say something. A light flickered on in her head and she wrapped an arm around Dirk's waist, returning the embrace from hell.

"Feels more like a couple of days."

Dirk exploded with clumsy laughter. He leaned over, kissing Laura on the lips. The kiss landed like a headbutt and Laura screamed inside. Dirk's lips were dry and his breath reeked of stale tobacco.

They were overdoing it.

"Where are the kids?" Dirk asked. There was a hopeful look on his face as he glanced over Court and Amir's shoulders, towards the open doorway. Clearly, the man expected his children to rush downstairs and throw themselves into Daddy's arms.

Except, Amir was Daddy now. And the house was silent.

"They're out," Court said. "With their friends."

Laura looked at the two upstairs windows. She wondered if the kids were up there somewhere, huddled together on the floor, hiding. Keeping quiet at their mother's instruction. That's what she would have done.

"They're out?"

Court nodded.

Dirk couldn't hide his disappointment. Soon, his eyes were black holes again. Locked on Court.

It was Amir, still blocking the entrance to the house, who spoke next. "Dirk, didn't we sort this out last time? Didn't we ask you to, umm, call before you came over to the house?"

Laura was still smiling. Her face was throbbing.

"I was just passing by," Dirk said, sounding deflated. He looked at Laura. "Isn't that right, darling? We were just–"

Laura nodded. She took the lead this time. Speaking in a bright, chirpy tone.

"We were having brunch in Partick. Down by the round-about there. Dirk had already mentioned that there were boxes that needed picking up. It was my idea to come over. Sorry for the inconvenience, but no point in Dirk's things taking up space, is there?"

Amir and Court exchanged tense looks.

"It's okay," Court said, taking a step back. Clearing a path for Dirk. "Get your boxes but after that, you call first. Got it? Amir's right. We spoke about this last time. No more surprise visits, at any hour of day."

Dirk was smiling again. "Cup of tea for Laura while she waits?"

"No," Laura said, throwing up her hands. "That's okay. I'm fine."

Dirk's jugular was back on full display.

"Have some tea."

"Really. It's not necessary"

"Okay."

Dirk gave Laura another nudge. He was as subtle as a sledgehammer to the skull. Felt like he was pushing her into the middle of the garden, towards Court. It was obvious what he wanted to happen. The two women, standing face to face. Laura clung to her smile. Shoved both hands into her pockets, trying to appear relaxed. Which of course, made her look anything but relaxed.

Dirk clicked his fingers. "Amir, help me get the boxes in the car, will you?"

Amir arched his eyebrows.

"Sure," he said, walking down the front steps. "I'll help you. Not like I was doing anything else, was it?"

Dirk walked past the women, making his way to the side of the house. He unlatched the wooden gate, pulled it open, and disappeared down the narrow path that led to the back garden. Amir trudged behind Dirk, giving Court a what-the-hell look before he was out of sight.

The two women were alone in the front garden.

Laura noticed movement at the window of the house across the street. A white-haired woman, in her sixties or seventies, was standing at the window. Peering out from behind the curtains. She disappeared after she realised Laura could see her.

Clearly, the old girl was expecting some action.

What had she seen before?

"*Would* you like a cup of tea?" Court asked. Her voice was softer. More relaxed in the absence of Dirk. "It's no problem."

"No thanks," Laura said. She found it hard to maintain eye contact with the other woman. This whole operation was about deceiving her after all. "I doubt we'll be staying very long. And again, I'm sorry about just turning up like this on a Sunday."

"That's okay."

Court looked over at the side gate. There was a hint of noise from the back of the house, but no sign of Dirk or Amir yet.

She smiled at Laura.

"So, how long have you known Dirk? Two weeks, was it?"

"Not long. It all happened very quickly."

Very quickly.

"He's done well for himself," Court said. In a split second, she looked Laura up and down. "I'm surprised. I didn't expect him to bounce back so quickly."

"Dirk's full of surprises."

"You can say that again."

Laura and Court made small talk while Dirk and Amir loaded seven cardboard boxes of varying sizes, all taped shut, into the boot and backseat of the Corolla. Dirk whistled while he worked. Doing his best to sound cheerful. Laura's smile had long since fizzled out. All her attempts at conversation were forced or ridiculous. She was polite however, and Court seemed intrigued by her presence.

Still, the plan wasn't working. A blind man could see that. Laura had never been good at telling fibs. Dirk was still overdoing it, walking over to Laura every time he saw her, giving her a kiss on the cheek while Court looked on. He called Laura 'honey', 'sweetheart' and 'baby'. Laura's skin crawled whenever he touched her. All she wanted to do was go home and have a shower. Wash it off. Wash *him* off.

Eventually, they said their goodbyes, and climbed back into the car. To Laura's surprise, Dirk was still whistling as they drove away from Medwyn Street.

"That went well," he said.

Laura wasn't about to argue, even if he was deluded. "So you'll keep your promise. You'll destroy the footage?"

"I'm a man of my word. You were brilliant back there. I'm getting my family back because of you."

Laura sat back, gazing out of the passenger side window. They passed the old school. The roundabout. Soon, they were back in Partick. Heading towards Byres Road. How could Dirk be so blind about what just happened?

"Will you drop me off at the nearest bus stop?" she asked.

Dirk's eyes were on the road. "I can do better than that. I'll take you back to Great Western Road."

Laura's fingers fidgeted with the shoulder strap of her bag. Despite her ordeal being almost over, she was filled with a sudden dread she couldn't understand. An impending sense of doom. Rising up. It was as if she'd seen something in the blink of an eye. A flicker of something terrible. A bleak future. But there was nothing. Only Dumbarton Road. Only the steady hum of the Corolla. The people of Glasgow walking on both sides of the street, going about their business.

She didn't want to be in a car with this man. Not for one second longer.

Laura declined the offer with a sweep of the hand.

"I'd prefer the bus stop."

6

She was glad to put the weekend behind her. Glad to be back at work on Monday morning, losing herself in the company's latest project – a set of horror props for a local Halloween theatre production.

There was still a lot of work to do and the props were due at the theatre by the end of the week. Laura was working on a set of mannequin heads (donated by a local clothes shop), covering them in glue and then applying paint to add the 'dead look' before adding the blood, bruises, the severed neck and finishing up each one with a wig.

The props were some of her best work to date. As Laura sat at her workbench, head down in concentration, some of the interns were lapping the studio, recording the creative process and posting the clips on Masons' Tik-Tok, Facebook and Instagram accounts. Masons were a modern entity. They were big on their social media presence, big to the point of obsession, and although the floating interns could be distracting, Laura was used to it.

Angela, a nineteen-year-old from Dublin, was standing

opposite Laura's desk. Holding her phone horizontally, capturing Laura's work for the camera. She inched closer. Clearly doing her best to be quiet.

Laura looked up. Gave Angela a smile.

"Alright?"

Angela nodded and smiled back. "You hear that?"

"Hear what?"

"Sounds like a phone buzzing under the desk."

Laura tilted her head. Sure enough, the muffled ringtone and buzz came from inside the set of drawers where she kept her general admin stuff.

"Yep. That's me."

"I thought so."

"I must have forgot to put it on silent," Laura said, downing tools and kicking her chair back a couple of inches.

She stood up, stretching her arms to get the blood flowing. Her joints clicked. She took off her gloves. After wiping her hands dry, Laura opened the top drawer and pulled out the phone. How many times had he called her today? Five? Six? Laura glanced at the oversized digital clock on the wall.

It was ten o'clock in the morning.

"Fuck."

"Someone's persistent," Angela said, pointing at the phone. "Aren't they? You think they might have given up by now."

"Sure are."

"Want me to answer it for you?" Angela said, reaching for the phone. "It's no problem. I'll tell whoever it is that you're busy."

"No, it's okay."

"I can tell them to fuck off if you'd prefer a less subtle approach?"

Laura smiled. "No thanks. I'd better get this. I'll take it out in the corridor."

"Okay," Angela said, setting off towards the next workbench to get some more Tik-Tok footage for the company.

Laura walked towards the double doors, her head spinning. She sped up. Face burning. Felt like some kind of panic attack coming on.

Was it obvious? Was anyone watching her?

A quick glance around the studio. Just a bunch of artists with their heads down, lost in work. Interns filming. No one was paying any attention to Laura.

She looked at the phone. She'd saved his number as 'Clinic' on Saturday, just in case Tommy happened to see it. Not much chance of that, but she couldn't take the risk. Over the past twenty-four hours, Laura had received a bunch of texts and missed calls from 'Clinic'. Too many. The calls started coming in at around nine o'clock last night. Why was he doing this? It was supposed to be over. She'd done everything he asked of her.

Now he was calling her at work?

Fuck.

Another favour, Laura thought. *He wants another favour.* What next? Double-dating with Court and Amir?

The phone was still ringing. That had to be three minutes now. Straight. Maybe more. Laura had turned off voicemail, but it was clear that Dirk wasn't going to hang up. Even if the call cut off, he'd dial again. And again.

She had to speak to him.

Laura pushed through the double doors, stepping out into the corridor. Without the air conditioning in the studio, it was cold. Her shoulders gave a little shudder. She stopped at the top of a set of green carpeted stairs that led down to reception.

Taking a deep breath, Laura hit the green button. Pressed the phone against her ear.

"Hello."

There was no answer at first. *He's hung up*, she thought. That wasn't any comfort because he was only going to keep calling and calling. Five minutes from now. Ten minutes. An hour. The creep wasn't going to go away.

What if he comes to the flat?

The thought made Laura sick. He *did* have her address. He was a Budz driver who was supposed to have taken her home on Friday night. He knew exactly where she lived. The street, the flat number, everything. It was all in her Budz account.

Laura made a fist. She was about to hit the wall when she heard a noise on the other end of the line. A rip. Sounded like fabric tearing inside her ear.

"Hello? Dirk? Are you there?"

Laboured breathing. Sounded painful, like the last gasp of a dying man. Then, it stopped. Followed by that bland, monotone voice that Laura had learned to dread over the course of a single weekend.

"Not answering my calls, hmm?"

She could almost smell the stale smoke.

"Why are you calling me, Dirk?"

"Ha! Why aren't you picking up?"

There was a strange tremor in his voice. Dirk wasn't in the same good headspace he'd been in when he dropped Laura off at the bus stop in Partick yesterday. That much was obvious. He'd even waved as he drove off. Wished her all the best. Like they were best pals.

"Dirk?"

"W-w-hy aren't you answering my calls? Why have you been ignoring me all morning?"

Laura spoke through gritted teeth. "I'm at work."

"Don't ignore me. Don't ever ignore me."

Laura sighed. She wanted to ask him if he'd deleted the footage. Kept up his end of the bargain. But she was too scared to know the answer. Maybe she knew already and didn't want to hear it.

Laura leaned her back against the wall, taking deep gulps of air. Beads of sweat had formed on her forehead. She wasn't cold anymore. The double doors to the studio were pushed open from the inside, making her jump. Kathy, one of the other artists, walked through the doorway. Probably on a toilet break. She waved at Laura. Laura waved back, waiting for Kathy to disappear downstairs before she continued talking.

"C'mon Dirk, this is too much. I did what you asked. I was with you at Court's house yesterday, remember? Why are you calling and texting me?"

That raspy breathing in her ear.

"Dirk?"

"You told her, didn't you?"

Laura flinched. He might as well have stabbed her through the earpiece with a knitting needle. "Dirk, what the hell are you talking about?"

"Don't lie to me."

Laura lowered her voice, well aware that Kathy would be coming back soon. "You're not making any sense."

He gasped. "You f-f-fucking c-c-c–"

"Dirk, woah! Please take it easy."

"When? When did you do it? You told her when I was in the shed, didn't you? You waited until I was out of sight, then you told her everything."

Laura took her back off the wall. She walked over to the staircase, legs starting to feel wobbly. Checked to see if anyone was coming upstairs. The coast was clear, for now. "Dirk, listen to me. You need to calm down."

That was the wrong thing to say. Who calmed down after being told to calm down?

"Admit it!" Dirk snapped.

"Admit what?"

"That you t-t-told her."

"Told her what? That it was all a lie? A sham? No, of course I didn't tell her. Think about it Dirk – what good would that do me? Court finding out. How does that help me erase the footage?"

"You hate me," he growled. "You want me humiliated."

Laura's fingers curled into a shaking fist. She thumped the top of the bannister. Unable to believe that she still had to deal with this obnoxious man-child. "I'll ask you again. How does it help me erase the footage? Which is all I care about by the way."

A pause.

"I thought it worked," Dirk said. His voice cracked with emotion. Went up in pitch. "I really thought I saw it in her eyes."

"Saw what?"

"R-r-regret."

Laura wiped the sweat off her brow. *Jesus.* Her throat was parched. She couldn't remember the last time she'd drank something. "Listen, Dirk. I thought it worked too. How do you know for sure that it didn't?"

"She just phoned me."

"And?"

Laura jammed her ear against the phone. There was a muffled noise in the background. A code of strange sounds that she couldn't decipher.

Was Dirk crying?

"Are you alright?" Laura asked.

Stupid question.

"When I saw her name on the phone," he said in a gargled voice. "When I saw that, I thought it had worked. I thought I was getting my family back."

He sounded exhausted. Like a man who hadn't slept in weeks.

"I can't live like this."

Laura could just imagine Dirk sitting in a dingy flat somewhere in Glasgow. Lights off. Stale smoke, overflowing ashtrays, empty bottles and takeaway boxes all over the floor. Waiting for the phone call that would turn his life around. He would have been ecstatic when Court finally rang. Maybe he even did a happy dance before answering.

And now this.

She heard a loud thump, like he'd flopped into a chair.

"Dirk?"

"She asked me where I got my fake girlfriend from. How much did I pay to have you standing beside me? *How much did you pay? How much did you pay?* Can you believe it? She thought I hired you off the internet."

Laura wondered what Court would say if she knew that Dirk had drugged, kidnapped, sexually manipulated and blackmailed her? Was that better than hiring someone off the internet?

Not a good time to ask.

"I'm sorry Dirk. I tried my best yesterday. Swear to God, I never said a word to Court about any of it, you know? We made small talk. I'm sure she was–"

"Enough."

The hiss was back in his voice. That frantic breathing in Laura's ear.

"Please talk to me, Dirk."

No answer.

Shit, Laura thought.

Kathy walked back upstairs, a cup of coffee in hand, steam billowing from inside. She looked surprised to see Laura still on the phone. Eyebrows up. Big smile. Laura waved, then quickly turned the other way, which might have come off as rude, but she didn't have time to be polite right now. Dirk was losing it. Really losing it. And that meant big trouble.

"Dirk?" she said, lowering her voice. "I know you're in pain right now. But listen to me, okay? Maybe–"

She hesitated. What was she supposed to say to this creep? Her mind was a blank, pulling out useless words from the void.

"Maybe what?" he asked.

"Maybe this is a good thing. Did you ever think about that? Sounds to me like Court's grilling you for information. She called you, didn't she? That's good. She reached out. You've touched a nerve. Maybe she really is jealous."

Silence.

"Dirk?"

Nothing.

"Dirk, are you still there?"

Laura heard a bellowing noise that chilled her blood. It sounded like an animal in pain. She wasn't sure if Dirk was even listening to her anymore.

"Dirk, what's going on? Talk to me."

The wounded animal was Dirk. And it sounded like he was having a major meltdown on the phone.

"DIRK!"

Laura stared at the phone in horror. It felt like the floor was opening up underneath her. The video footage. Had Dirk deleted it?

Don't be stupid, she thought. *Your life is in the hands of a madman. Now you're going to lose it all. Tommy. Work. Everything.*

Laura's heart was racing, but she managed to speak in a soft, calm voice. It sounded convincing. Sincere. "Please Dirk. Let's talk."

"She's laughing at me."

There it was. His voice, a bitter and distorted growl. But he was still there on the other end of the line, still talking. He hadn't slit his wrists or put a gun to his head.

Would that be such a bad thing?

"She's supposed to be angry. She's supposed to be spitting mad and instead, she's l-l-laughing at me. Her and Amir. Laughing all night on the couch. Laughing in bed after they've fucked. And you know what? The kids *were* in the house yesterday morning. I'm sure of it. I'd bet my life on it. She's hiding them from me. Hiding our children from their father."

Laura heard him take frantic gulps of air. Like he was drowning. The words spilled out in between.

"Why is she doing this to me?"

Laura's heart drummed in her chest. What now? How to fix this? She had to say something. Self-preservation was all that mattered now. To hell with this man and his problems. *His* problems. He was a monster and the truth was that he deserved to die alone.

Go on, she thought. *Put a rope around your neck.*

"Dirk? You believe me, don't you? I didn't tell her anything."

The voice that cut her off was distorted with rage. Laura took her phone off the earpiece and grimaced.

"I told you. Didn't I? I told you what would happen."

"Please."

"What, you didn't believe me? Didn't think I'd go through with it?"

Laura's legs were rooted to the spot. She felt dizzy. She reached for the bannister, worried she might fall. "You're scaring me."

"You should be scared."

"Why? I did what you asked, remember?"

Dirk sounded out of breath. "You gave her a signal, didn't you? You gave it away. What did you do?"

"I did nothing," Laura said.

"Tell me the truth and I'll delete the footage."

Laura struggled to keep her voice down. "You were supposed to have deleted it already, remember? Listen to me. I can't control what Court thinks. She didn't buy it, well too bad. It's not because of me. Not because of anything I did."

"I told you."

Panic shot through her veins. She should've gone to the police. As soon as she walked out of that hotel on Saturday morning, she should've gone to the police. Done it that way. Told them everything. Put everything out there, the kidnapping, the blackmail, all of it. Yes, there was the footage. And she'd be taking her chances with Tommy, the family and all her friends seeing it. But she wouldn't be in this situation now. With a psycho like Dirk threatening to ruin her.

They'd have believed her, wouldn't they?

Family. Friends. Tommy.

Why did she doubt them?

"I told you what would happen," Dirk said.

"Wait. Please."

Laura heard a sharp click in her ear. Followed by silence. "Dirk!"

She fell back against the wall. Stared at the iPhone in horror. Like it had just sprouted fangs.

He'd hung up on her.

"Oh no."

Deep breaths, she told herself. Gotta slow that heart down. Laura didn't know what she was supposed to do next. The choices didn't appeal. Fall into the depths of despair. Wait for Dirk to call her back. Tell someone. Wait for someone to get in touch and tell her that they'd just received an email from some guy called Dirk. That there was a link. A video.

"Fuck."

Laura buried her face in her hands.

Think it through, she thought. *Stay calm.* Dirk was angry. He was furious and insane. His plan, which had always been a terrible one, hadn't gone his way. Still, there was no way he'd go through with the threat. Was there? What did the self-obsessed psycho gain from posting the footage, sending it to Laura's family, friends and work colleagues?

Nothing. It was an idle threat. A threat he'd used to get Laura to play ball. He wasn't going to do anything. Most likely, she'd never hear from him again.

He was just lashing out.

But what if he did post it?

Laura was ruined.

What did she know about him? What could she tell anyone about the man who'd set her up? He was a Budz driver who drove a red Toyota Corolla. *Wow, don't hold back on the details.* Why hadn't she jotted down his registration plate? Or memorised it. Stupid. No, it was okay because Dirk wouldn't post the footage. He wouldn't risk going to prison because if that happened, he really would lose everything, including his kids.

Laura closed her eyes. Saw Dirk's home movie playing in her mind. There she was, a drunken mess, lying naked on the bed. Laughing. Her eyes spinning like flying saucers.

There'd be no sympathy for her. None. She was the woman who had it all, a nice flat, great fiancée, and a great career. Someone who had everything going for her and she'd ruined it by having a stupid one-night stand. That's what it looked like.

She'd tell them it never happened.

They wouldn't believe her.

Her stomach lurched.

Laura moved away from the wall, staring at the phone. Would he call her back? She thought about calling him first. There had to be a way to fix this. Maybe she could arrange a meeting with Dirk later that day and they could talk it through face to face. Whatever black cloud hung over him, it might have shifted by them. They had to talk. Work something out. Maybe he'd take some money after all.

"Fuck it," she said, scrolling to contacts. She tapped her thumb off the screen.

It went straight to Dirk's voicemail. That monotone voice sent a shiver down her spine.

If you'd like to leave your name and number, I'll get back to you as soon as possible.

Laura shoved the phone back in her pocket. She paced the landing, trying to burn off some of that nervous energy. None of this was in her control. Her fate was in the hands of a heartbroken lunatic.

It felt like she was falling. Like it had begun.

No, she reminded herself. He wouldn't release the footage.

She tried to bring herself back to this safe space. He wouldn't do it. All this worry, it was for nothing. It was silly.

"Get back to work," she said out loud. "Stay busy. Think of something else."

In a week, she'd have forgotten all about it. All about Dirk, who'd finally move on with his life or with any luck, he'd swallow a bottle of pills or jump off a tall building. There was no way he was going to ruin Laura's life, just because his marriage was over.

Okay, she thought. *It's going to be okay.*

Laura wiped the sweat off her face. She pushed the double doors open. Walked back into the studio with a smile on her face.

Those Halloween props weren't going to finish themselves.

PART II

THE HIGHLANDS

FIVE YEARS LATER

7

DIRK

"I win, Dad!"

Joe threw down the PlayStation controller and jumped up to his feet. He charged across the living room towards his stepdad, who was sitting opposite the TV. Dirk howled with laughter as Joe cupped his hands over his mouth and made the crowd-goes-wild-noise. The boy slammed into Dirk like a miniature rugby player.

"Beat you again!"

"Take it easy," Dirk said, catching a hold of the hyperactive child. "I'm not as robust as I used to be." They began to play-box, a familiar routine. Dirk threw a jab and Joe came back with a flurry of wild punches that hit air.

"I beat you!" Joe said, turning back to the TV. He pointed at the evidence on the TV screen, reminding everyone yet again that he'd defeated Dirk in another round of *Gran Turismo 7*. The split screen showed that Joe had completed the required thirty laps in record time while Dirk wasn't even close to finishing his set. Now that he'd lost, Dirk had no plans to finish either. He put down his controller on the armrest, conceding defeat.

"You're not getting any better, Dad."

"That's a matter of opinion."

"Nope. You're just really bad."

"Okay."

"Didn't you used to drive cars for a living?" Joe asked, running a hand through his sandy brown hair, a dishevelled mop that covered most of his face.

Dirk laughed. "I wasn't a Formula One driver."

"Wanna go again?"

"Give your dad a break," Diana said, looking up from her book. "He's been playing that game with you for almost two hours straight."

It was the first time she'd spoken in an hour. While the boys had been playing video games, Diana was stretched out on the couch, bare feet propped up against the armrest. Reading a Karin Slaughter novel.

"Maybe it's time for something else," she said. "Let me think. How about you start packing for the trip?"

Joe rolled his eyes. "It's too late to start packing now."

Diana gave her son a hard stare, lowering the book until it was flat on her chest. "Oh well. If it's too late to pack, it's too late to play games."

A loud groan from the boy.

"No."

"Tell me something. Have you even *started* packing for this trip yet?"

Joe made another soft groaning noise.

"I didn't think so," Diana said. "You do realise we're leaving in two days, don't you? Two days, Joe. It's not a lot of time to get ready. I thought you said you didn't want me to pack your bag for you anymore?"

Joe's face recoiled in horror. "I don't."

Diana stared at her son. The unflinching gaze of a mother who knew she couldn't lose.

"Know what I'm thinking? Right now, I'm thinking that I'll finish this chapter and then I'll go up to your room and make a start on packing your little bag. That means going through your wardrobe, through the drawers, you know? Still, I'm sure you've got nothing to hide."

Joe's face was as white as a sheet.

"Isla hasn't packed either," he said, pointing to the ceiling. A confident smile emerged on the boy's face as if he'd pulled out an ace.

His older sister, Isla, had been up in her room all night, most likely lying on the bed with her face glued to her iPhone. Getting in as much alone time as she needed before being stuck in a campervan with her parents and younger brother for a fortnight.

Diana batted away Joe's feeble excuse.

"You let me worry about Isla. Okay, smartie pants? Just start packing. And if you haven't made a start before bedtime, you won't be taking that handheld Nintendo with you."

"PlayStation Portable," Dirk said, cutting in. He smiled, but it was a little annoying how his wife always got the little details wrong when it came to video games. He sensed she was doing it deliberately.

Diana threw him a furious look across the living room.

"I don't care what it's called. Two weeks, remember? Pack accordingly and make sure you've got enough clothes for two weeks. We'll be up in the Highlands, living out of a campervan. No hotels. No luxury."

"Can I play one more game?" Joe asked.

"Upstairs. Start packing."

Joe gave Dirk a desperate look. The boy was seeking out allies. Reinforcements.

Dirk's response was a casual shrug of the shoulders. "Sorry, Joe. Better do what the boss lady says."

Joe stood up. Gave the TV a pitiful look. "We need to get some new games."

No response from the adults.

"Someone in school said that *Ghostwire: Tokyo* is amazing. It's got great reviews on all the gaming websites. How about this? If I promise to finish packing by tomorrow afternoon, can we buy the game?"

Diana let out a single scoffing laugh. "Did you hear what I said? Just pack your bloody bag, will you?"

She pointed at the open door, towards the stairs.

"Our boy's a tough negotiator," Dirk said. "Wonder who he gets that from, eh?"

Diana smiled. She found her bookmark on the floor, slipped it into the page, then closed the book over. Then, she picked up another book. This was a slim, glossy-looking travel guide about the North Coast 500 road trip. Diana had been reading it in advance of the family's campervan holiday.

"The ultimate road trip in the Scottish Highlands."

There was always a smile on her face when she read aloud from the book. Her voice softened, like she was recording a chocolate commercial. "The NC500 is a road trip that's as much about the journey as it is about the destination."

"What *is* the destination?" Joe asked.

Diana ignored him. Took a sip of hot chocolate, then continued to read aloud.

"Windswept beaches, ancient castles and ruins and there's a lot more that the stunning landscape has to offer in the far north of Scotland. Drive from Inverness up the east coast to John o' Groats and then back down the west coast, returning to Inverness. Or go the other way. The options are limitless."

Limitless, Dirk thought. He liked the sound of that.

It was her idea for the family to travel the NC500. A longstanding dream that went back decades, but her previous husband, Alan, had only ever wanted beaches and sunshine for his holidays. Alan wasn't one to think outside the box. He *was* the box. And he usually got what he wanted. That was one of the reasons that Diana had eventually left him, taking their two children with her.

One of many reasons.

Dirk, on the other hand, was happy to encourage Diana's dream of more adventurous holidays. He liked to think of himself as a supportive husband. Something Court had taken for granted back in the day. They'd been working hard. They deserved a break and this was a great way to see more of that picture postcard Scotland they both loved. Dirk had been left in charge of hiring the campervan and he was pleased with his choice, a Fiat Ducato that slept four and had everything they needed – beds, kitchen, bathroom, and living space. It wasn't cheap but at least they weren't forking out for flights or over-priced hotel rooms.

"Dad?" Joe said. "What do you think about *Ghostwire*?"

Diana wasn't about to let anyone else speak. "Those games cost a fortune. Fifty quid for a bloody computer game? Do you think I'm made of money, Joe?"

Joe's shoulders sagged. A sure sign of defeat.

"But..."

Dirk pointed at the door. "Go upstairs and start packing. Just make a start, you don't have to do it all tonight. And who knows? When we get back from the trip, maybe we'll talk about *Ghostwire*, okay?"

Diana's eyebrows stood up. But she didn't say anything.

Joe trudged out of the living room with all the enthusiasm of someone walking towards the guillotine. Dirk stood up, picking up the PlayStation controllers and putting them back in the drawer under the TV.

"Game over," he said.

Diana nodded. "Thank God."

Dirk fell back into the armchair, opening up his laptop. He browsed a few video game outlets and looked up *Ghostwire*, researching where he could get it cheapest. Cheap was still expensive. Still, it *would* be a nice present for Joe when they came back from the Highlands, assuming the boy was on his best behaviour. That meant not complaining. Not fighting with his sister.

Dirk tried to play it cool as he browsed the different online stores. He didn't want Diana to know that *he* wanted the game every bit as much as Joe did.

Let the boy do all the heavy lifting.

Eventually, after making a few notes, he closed the tab.

There was another tab still open. The tab with the articles he'd been reading last night. About the woman. The woman they called *The Don't Drink Girl*.

Dirk glanced at Diana. His face felt like it was on fire, but she was too absorbed in the book to notice him blushing. He looked back at the screen. Clicked the tab. Why had he typed 'Don't Drink Girl' into the search bar last night? He'd been sitting downstairs in the living room alone, sinking a couple of beers (that was his limit these days) while Diana and the kids were upstairs watching a talent contest on ITV. Junk. The sort of thing he couldn't stand. Something led Dirk to think about her. About what he'd done. Where was she now? What was she doing with herself since becoming a meme? There were plenty of images on Google – stills taken from his original footage in that hotel room. He'd last typed 'Don't Drink Girl' into the search bar two years ago. A lot of new ones had gone up since then.

Memes. Videos. Photos. So many photos.

Another glance at Diana. Absorbed in her book, her lips moving as she read in silence.

His eyes skimmed the photos.

The blonde woman lying naked on a bed. Eyes closed, beads of sweat gathering on her forehead. That killer smile. White teeth. It looked like she was having the time of her life and yet Dirk knew better. He'd made it look convincing. This image and hundreds more had been lifted from a series of video highlights that went viral five years ago. Highlights, skilfully edited down to about a minute of footage. *One minute and three seconds*, Dirk thought.

Enough time to ruin a life.

He shifted in the armchair. There was a rush of excitement in his veins that he hadn't expected.

He did that. All of it.

The ceiling groaned above his head. A thump. Sounded like Joe dropping his suitcase on the floor.

Dirk turned his attention back to the laptop.

The poor bitch had become a warning for women everywhere. *Look what happens to good girls who drink too much. You don't want to end up like the Don't Drink Girl, do you? Don't want to become a meme.* Look at her. Her real name was rarely if ever mentioned these days. Dirk couldn't even remember her real name. It began with a–

Nope, it was gone. It had been too long.

Poor bitch.

She'd become a symbol.

Dirk wiped his brow dry with the back of his hand. Slowly. That rush of excitement again. The power. Was he supposed to feel bad about what happened to her? Guilty?

If so, it wasn't there.

A good thing, he told himself. If nothing else, she'd set an example and one that would keep other young women like Isla out of trouble. God knows, young women were running wild these days. Most of them were lost, aspiring to live fake Instagram lives. Obsessed with image and ridiculous beauty standards.

The Don't Drink Girl might put a few of them off alcohol and drugs. If so, then it was worth it. It was a public service.

What was *her* name?

Dirk had never expected it to blow up like this. Not in a million years could he have predicted what would happen. The only time in his life anything had gone viral. And he got no credit for it. Typical. Still, that was a long time ago. Things were different now. *Much* different. He had Diana, Isla and Joe. There was no way he'd ever crack the way he'd cracked back then. No way he'd resort to doing the sort of things he'd done.

He wasn't the same man anymore.

It was a long road back after Court left him. All he'd wanted to do was die, but he was too scared to actually kill himself. But he *was* prepared to drink himself to death. Nice and slow. Didn't matter to Dirk how long it took. About three weeks later, a chance encounter in the local park changed everything. He'd been sitting on the bench by the boating pond. Watching the swans. Enjoying a rare moment of peace. A woman sat down beside him and started throwing a mixture of seeds onto the path for the birds. There was something about the woman that drew him in. Electricity. Chemistry. Magic. An easy conversation followed. Dirk's stammer, which often appeared whilst talking to women, wasn't there. There were no awkward silences. What did he have to lose? He asked her out and Diana, for reasons he would never understand, said yes.

Court. His biological kids. Glasgow.

All that was behind him.

He lived in Edinburgh now, working with his father-in-law in the furniture-selling business. Dirk enjoyed the work. It was easy. He liked the customers. Anything was better than the crappy driving jobs he'd done for so long. All those late nights. Soulless existence. All the shit he'd taken from people who treated him like he was invisible.

Never again.

Best of all, he was a father again. Diana's kids loved him and they called him Dad. They didn't even call their biological father Dad. They called him Alan.

A stable family.

That's all Dirk had ever wanted. Something far removed from the narcissistic mother and alcoholic father he'd grown up with in the Netherlands. A nice home with no shouting. No intimidation. No fear, no humiliation tactics. And with Court, he'd done that. He'd created bliss, then she took it away from him. She took his children and gave them to Amir. She didn't want to know him. Tried to keep the children away from Dirk, implying that he wasn't safe to be around. That he was unstable. A danger to his own children.

The fucking nerve.

Yes, he'd gone to the edge. He'd kidnapped a woman. Stripped her. Blackmailed her. He'd tried it a few times before the Don't Drink Girl, but his nerve had always failed him. It took three failed attempts before going through with it. *What a mess*, he thought. All to make his wife jealous. That had failed too. So, he'd lashed out at the gorgeous

blonde. Posted the footage on multiple social media plat-
forms via dummy accounts. Emailed her fiancée. Her
employer. Turned her into an instant meme.

Poor bitch.

He looked at the 'Don't Drink Girl' on Google Images.
So many of them.

What *was* her name again?

With a sigh, he closed the laptop lid over. Sat in silence.
Then, he glanced at Diana. God, he was so lucky to have a
woman like that in his life. The sort of strong-willed woman
he loved. Forty-years old, intelligent and a great mother.
Selfless, nothing like his own monstrosity of a mother.
Diana was the type of woman who'd die to protect her
family.

"You're looking at that game," Diana said, snapping the
travel book shut. "The one Joe wants. Aren't you?"

"Nope."

"Dirk..."

He shook his head.

"Actually, I was just checking some things off the holiday
list. We still don't have an ice box for the campervan,
do we?"

8

LAURA

Customers.

Laura saw them coming, but stayed at the edge of the road. She watched as the silver Audi slowed down, pulling off the A9, swerving into the lay-by where Laura's red and white campervan was parked.

"Morning."

She gave them a wave. Took one last drag of the cigarette, knelt down and stubbed it out onto the road. She put the mangled butt in her back pocket. She'd keep it there until she found a bin.

Laura stood up, patting down her shirt and jeans. Fragments of dust and dirt showered off her clothes.

The Audi driver turned the engine off. The car doors opened, front and back. Two blonde teenage girls and a younger girl of about ten, with mousy-brown hair, stepped out of the back, taking in their surroundings with confused, fearful expressions, as if they'd just set foot on an alien planet. A man and a woman, both in their early-to-mid forties, followed the girls out of the car. The woman was tall and leggy, with black hair. Laura was reminded of an actress. What's-her-name? Anjelica Huston. The man was hefty around the middle with a thick, Selleck-like moustache that belonged in the eighties.

"Good afternoon," the woman said.

American.

This could be good, Laura thought. The Americans liked throwing their money around. Especially when it came to supporting local artists who hadn't showered in a week.

Laura waved again. "Hi."

"Nice office you got here. Fresh air. A gorgeous view. Beats the hell out of any office I've ever worked in."

"I like it," Laura said, laughing. "No complaints, not at this time of year anyway. Winter? Not so great."

This particular spot on the A9 was one of her favourite pitches. She was about three miles outside the town of Invergordon. There were green fields to the front and back. A scattering. of houses. Beyond the houses to the front, a dark green hill sprouted like a giant tortoise shell.

"We saw the sign about a half mile back," the woman said, approaching Laura with an outstretched hand. "Thought we might have missed you."

Laura took the woman's hand. Felt a strong grip.

"Here I am."

The woman looked down at the jewellery trays lined up in the lay-by. Three rows of three, nine containers in total. Her eyes lit up.

"Oh wow! These are so freaking cool. What kind of bracelets do you have?"

"Woven ones. I've got plenty of beaded necklaces out today too. If you're into that kind of thing."

The woman's voice jumped an octave. Her excitement

was theatrical, but it seemed genuine. "You bet I am. These are just gorgeous. Do you mind if the girls and I browse for a little while?"

Laura stepped aside, giving the family some room. "Take your time."

She retreated back to the campervan. Looked at her cracked phone screen while the woman and three girls browsed the jewellery trays, oohing and aahing like they were looking at the cutest puppies ever. The man stood back, clearly not interested in bracelets and necklaces. There was a stoic, neutral expression on his face. Polite boredom. At the same time, he inched closer to Laura. Shuffled around. Shoved his hands deep into his pockets and gave her an awkward smile.

"Make these yourself?"

Laura nodded. "I do."

"Where do you get the materials?"

"Local suppliers. Wherever I can get them."

"That your studio back there?"

He pointed at the van.

"Sometimes. If I'm not on the move, I work at a friend's house. She lives nearby and I'll stay with her a day or two while I get the stock levels back up. Apart from that, I'm on the road."

"Friend, huh? She the famous one who lives around here? The one all the true crime junkies go mad for?"

"No, that's not her."

He nodded. "Are you from around here?"

"Yeah. Local girl."

That was the stock answer, even if it wasn't true. Nobody needed to know where Laura was from. Besides, people went nuts for the word 'local'.

The man took a step back, looking both ways down the road. "Do you get a lot of people pulling over?"

"Most days it's good," Laura said. "I like to switch it up between various pitches, especially at this time of year. The NC500 is always crawling with-"

"Tourists?"

He was grinning.

Laura grinned back. "Pretty much."

The conversation fizzled out. The man shuffled off again, kicking up a cloud of dust at the side of the road. He pulled out his phone. Walked back towards the car, scraping the sole of his boot off the asphalt like a bored child waiting for a parent that forgot to pick him up. Meanwhile, the woman and three girls shopped. Laura kept out of the way. She didn't mind the wait. Active customers made the roadside pitch look attractive.

A couple of cars did go past, travelling north. Nobody stopped. Laura listened to the sound of their engines fading into the distance.

"We'll take all of these," the woman said, walking over to Laura after about ten minutes of shopping in total. The girls were standing behind their mother. They had more bracelets and necklaces in their hands than Laura had sold in the past week.

She played it cool.

"Great," Laura said. "So glad you found something."

The woman nodded. "They're just so gorgeous. We've picked out plenty for ourselves and we're going to give some to friends and family as birthday and holiday gifts when we get back to the US. It's okay to buy this much, right? We're not leaving you with nothing else to sell?"

"Buy as much as you want. And thank you."

"Thank you for being so friggin' talented, huh?"

Laura smiled. How many of those bracelets and necklaces would end up gathering dust in a cardboard box? What did it matter? She was getting paid. The Americans were buying a *lot* of stuff. Was it a charity purchase? Did Angelica Huston pity her? Laura wouldn't have been surprised. She was no longer the glamorous, well-dressed woman she'd once been. Her clothes were old and faded. So was her face. She looked ten years older than her age. At least, that's what she told herself when she bothered to look in the mirror. She didn't wear makeup and her hair was cut short, dyed blue to hide the natural blonde colour. The old Laura was gone. Dead and buried. Now, she was just another poor artist, trying to scrape a living at the side of the road.

"Let me put those in a bag for you," she said to the woman.

"Paper?"

"I only use paper bags."

"Awesome."

Laura walked over to the van. Pulled the double doors open. She grabbed a large paper bag out of the supplies crate and held it open, allowing the Americans to drop their bracelets and necklaces in one at a time. Fourteen items in total. Not a bad day's work. She'd already sold a few necklaces earlier in the day to two English students on a road trip. Seventeen items in total. She could call it a day and it was still early.

Laura folded the paper bag over. Added some sellotape to hold it.

"All yours."

The woman was beaming. Her flawless white teeth on full display. God, the Americans loved their white teeth. Her husband and their children were already back at the Audi.

The girls had mumbled a brief but polite goodbye to Laura. Now, they were all inside the car. The engine was ticking over. Waiting for *Mom*.

"I love what you're doing here," the woman said, rummaging around in her tote bag for her purse. "This is so damn beautiful. Getting the fuck out of the rat race. Living life, you know? You're not selling tacky garbage either. This is real. I love to support *real* artists when I visit new places."

Laura smiled. "It's real alright."

The woman opened her purse. Pulled out a hundred-pound note. She looked at its markings, trying to decipher the strange patterns. "Will this cover it?"

"That more than covers it," Laura said.

"Spoken like a true artist. Take it. Keep the change honey."

"Wow. Are you sure?"

"I'm sure. And, if I may, let me give you a little piece of advice. You should think about getting a contactless card reader. Not that many people carrying cash around anymore. Not these days."

Laura gave an appreciative nod of the head. "Thanks. I'll get around to doing that, sooner or later."

"Worth thinking about," the woman said. "So, do you live on the road?"

"I do," Laura said, pocketing the hundred-pound note before the woman changed her mind. It felt heavy in her pocket. A good heavy. "Mostly, I'm in the van. Sometimes, I park up at local campsites. Other times, I stay at a friend's house. I was just telling your husband the same thing."

The woman's bronzed face glowed with admiration. "Nothing like the freedom of the road, is there? Did you grow up with hippies?"

Laura shook her head. "Far from it."

"What made you do it then?" the woman asked. "What made you go for the nomadic lifestyle?" She waved to her family, letting them know she was coming. The man waved back, his neutral expression unchanged. The Tom Selleck on his face was twitching though.

"I always liked the idea of owning a campervan," Laura said. "And having the freedom that came with it. I thought I'd do it when I was older."

She shrugged.

"Circumstances made it happen sooner."

"Awesome."

The woman held up her hand for a high-five. Laura obliged.

"Good for you. I'm envious. If I didn't have those girls to look after, well, I'll say no more than that, huh? Anyway, I'd better get going. Much to see, much to do."

The woman set off towards the car. She turned back, calling out to Laura.

"Maybe I'll see you on the road."

Laura felt the afternoon sun tickling the back of her neck. "Maybe."

A lot of customers said that. Laura never saw any of them again. There was a lot of road on the NC500 to get lost in.

"Enjoy the sights," she said.

The woman waved, then climbed back into the car.

The Audi rolled away with a cheerful toot of the horn. Laura waved one last time, then she walked back into the lay-by, pulling her phone out of her pocket. She'd felt it buzzing twice during her conversation with Angelica Huston. She glanced at the screen.

Two missed calls from her parents.

They'd tried calling her several times during the week. Made about five attempts in total now. Five or six.

The nerve. After all this time. After what they said to her back then.

Laura pushed back the surge of anger. It would be okay as long as she didn't think too much about it. Easier said than done.

She deleted the recent notifications and started to pack up her things.

9

LAURA

Laura spent the night in a nearby car park.

It was at the back of an old football pitch, no longer in use. In the years since its closure, the old car park had become something of an unofficial stopover site, used by tourists and truckers and anyone else in the know.

Laura ate baked beans on toast for dinner, drank two glasses of cheap wine and fell asleep in front of the TV. A typical night on the road. She barely managed to stub out her last cigarette in the glass before her eyes closed.

She woke up early, sluggish and stiff. Instant coffee. Cold water over the face. After putting on a fresh t-shirt and the same old jeans she'd been wearing for weeks, Laura drove the campervan to a ramshackle old farmhouse outside Alness, about twenty miles north of Inverness. It was a remote location, plenty of solitude and silence. Only the occasional hum of distant traffic. The farmhouse was like a second home to Laura, the place she came to recharge after a long stint on the road.

She drove off the A9, steering her Volkswagen Grand California through the open gateway and along the dirt-track driveway that wound its way to the house. The California's tyres crunched over the gravel. Cutting over the surface. Laura pulled up outside the house and a second later, the front door opened.

Roz Clarke appeared in the doorway, wiping her hands with a dishtowel. She waved, then walked over as Laura turned off the engine.

"Hello beautiful," Roz said, grinning. "Welcome back."

Laura stepped outside. The morning air was cool on her face. Once, she would have been worried about the sun and covered herself in all kinds of creams to protect her skin. That was a long time ago. That was someone else.

"Hey Roz."

The two women hugged, always a challenge for Laura. She had to stand on her tiptoes to reach Roz, a giant of a woman. Forty-seven years old. Well over six feet tall without shoes. Roz was a beautiful woman, even with all the lines on her face. Maybe because of them. Long grey hair, always tied back in a ponytail. Sharp blue eyes. A standard English accent with hints of the Highland lilt creeping in.

"How's it going honey?" Roz asked, letting go of Laura.

"I'm okay."

Roz looked at her. Narrowed her eyes.

"Nope. Something's wrong."

Laura walked towards the house. Roz followed her, catching up in a few giant strides over the gravel.

"Seriously, what is it?"

"Nothing."

"Oh Laura. If you can't tell me, who can you tell?"

Laura sighed. "My parents have been trying to call me."

"Oh. That's bad, is it?"

"I've been getting missed calls from them all week."

"Ahh," Roz said, nodding. "Missed calls or ignored calls?"

"Both."

Roz knelt down on the path, pulling up a few weeds that had sprouted alongside the driveway. There were so many that the impromptu gardening session made little difference. She scrunched them up in her hands, like she was trying to make a ball.

"So why aren't you picking up?"

Laura pulled a face. Like it was a dumb question. "We've got nothing to talk about."

"You hungry?" Roz asked, pointing towards the house. "I've got homemade soup on the boil if you want to hang around?"

Laura was shaking her head before the question was over. She stared over the grass, down towards the road. Enjoyed that fluttering breeze again. Imagined it was just for her.

"No thanks."

"You sure?"

"Yep. I just wanted to grab some material before hitting the road. Had a big sale yesterday. Cleaned me out. Looks like I'm going to have to stop putting off the creative work if I want to have anything to sell."

"You don't sound very enthusiastic," Roz said. "You used to love making those necklaces."

"I know."

Roz smiled. "You can still eat breakfast with me, can't you?"

"I can't stop, Roz."

Roz let go of the crumpled weeds, letting them scatter. "You can't outrun those missed calls either, honey. You know?"

Laura kicked the dirt at her feet. Went back to staring at the road.

"Pretty sure I can."

"Look at you," Roz said, eyes running over Laura's figure. "You're wasting away to nothing."

"Thanks Mum."

"I'm serious, honey. You're not eating enough. Stay for breakfast."

"I just want to keep moving," Laura said. "But I'll grab something to eat. Maybe I'll go down to Skiach. Been a while since I've been down there and it's a good place to start another loop of the tourist trail."

"Go there."

"I will."

"Promise?"

"Promise."

Roz looked at her, nodding. "So, what else is happening? Anything else bothering you besides family stuff?"

Laura leaned against the house. Touched the phone through her pocket, hoping it wouldn't vibrate. "Nope. It's just the arrogance, you know? They treat me like shit, ignore me and then all of a sudden, they–"

"Yeah?"

"Fuck it. I need to blow off some steam."

"What did you have in mind?"

Laura smiled. "Too early to shoot cans?"

Roz whistled. "Ooh, honey. There *is* something wrong isn't there? Usually, I'm the one to suggest a little therapeutic shooting. And no, it's never too early. Or late for that matter. No neighbours to worry about around here."

That's what Laura wanted to hear.

"I'll get my rifle," she said, taking her back off the house.

She walked over to the campervan, opened up the back doors and pulled out the Remington 700. A recent model with a stainless-steel barrel. She'd bought the gun for safety reasons four years ago. A lone woman travelling around the Highlands needed protection. Better safe than sorry. She took lessons. Got good and even enjoyed it.

Roz was waiting at the back of the farmhouse, which was open space for miles. She'd lined up the targets. Empty beer cans on wooden crates. There was little talking and the two women went at it, taking it in turns to shoot. The rifle crack was a satisfying jolt. Better than any therapist, as far as Laura was concerned. Exactly what she needed in that moment. It was either that or start a fight with a stranger. The whip-like shots drifted for miles over an endless green landscape while up above, the morning sun soaked the sky blood-orange.

Laura's aim was off. She was missing a hell of a lot more than she was hitting. Missing badly. After about ten minutes of shooting, she called it a day.

"Damn it."

She took a step back, scolding herself for a piss poor showing.

"Feeling any better?" Roz asked.

"Nah."

"Not to worry. We all have our off days."

The way Roz said it. Not just a meaningless, well-intended turn of phrase. Something she knew. Something she'd lived. Right there in her eyes. She leaned her rifle against the house. Walked through the back door, returning soon afterwards with two cans of cold beer.

"Breakfast is served."

Roz pulled the tabs on both cans. Handed one to Laura. Beer for breakfast wasn't unusual at Roz's place. It was the standard delicacy, along with a neverending supply of cigarettes. The two women sat down on the grass, leaning their backs against the farmhouse. Looking out towards the road. The hazy morning was silent, except for the occasional flap of wings as a bird flew over the roof.

"You cold?" Roz asked. "Want a blanket or something?"

"I'm alright."

Laura sipped her beer. That first taste was sensational. And it was cold – even colder than she'd been expecting. "How are you anyway?"

Roz shrugged. "Bit of a rough night."

"What happened?"

"Don't worry about it. Couldn't sleep. It's always hard when I can't sleep and I end up just lying there in bed. Thinking. Sweating."

"Shit."

"Never mind me," Roz said. "Family stuff that bad, is it?"

Laura's sluggish nod of the head said it all. "It's really pissing me off and I wish I just didn't give a shit. That's what they deserve."

"So, you don't know what's up?"

"Nope."

"You'll find out if you talk to them."

"Seriously?"

"That bad, eh?"

"Yes, it was. If they're so ashamed of me, so disgusted by what happened, why don't they keep pretending like I don't exist? At this stage, I think it's best we just go on the way we are."

"Have you spoken to them since you left?" Roz asked.

Laura shrugged. "About three or four times. And it's always been me who made the effort. I'm the one who makes sure we have our contact numbers up-to-date, just in case, you know? Shouldn't have bothered. They didn't even tell me when my Aunt Susan died three years ago. I fucking loved that woman. But fine, I accepted it. The damage was done and we were out of each other's lives. I got used to it. Now, they're calling me?"

"Maybe something's happened, honey."

Laura shook her head. "They'd leave a voice message. Or a text."

Roz drank the beer like it was lemonade on a hot day. She leaned back, stretched out her long legs. Her clothes were worn and faded like Laura's. Tattered sweater with loose threads. Ripped jeans. They were a couple of tramps in the middle of nowhere, sitting on the grass, sipping cold beers with their rifles at hand.

"I know we always said we'd never talk about the lives we left behind," Roz said. "But if you want to–"

Laura smirked. "Do *you* want to?"

"Oh honey. You know more about my life than I know about yours. My life's an open book."

"I don't know about that, Roz. What are you thinking about when you're lying awake at night?"

"We could just forget about talking altogether," Roz said quickly. "There's plenty of beer in the fridge. I've got weed and mushrooms to last for days. We could just go to outer space for a while. A three-day bender, what do you say?"

"I'm not staying. Can't get wasted."

"Suit yourself."

They were silent for a moment. Then, Laura started talking. Opening those locked doors in her mind.

"I walked out of a pub in Glasgow five years ago," she said. "I used a ridesharing app to get home. The driver drugged me."

Roz reached over. Gave Laura's arm a squeeze.

"Fucking bastard."

"Yep."

Laura felt a cold tingling sensation. She looked up, checking for a pack of rogue clouds blocking the sun. There were none and yet, the light around the farmhouse had dimmed. It felt more like dusk than dawn.

"He took me to a hotel."

Roz's face hardened. "Oh shit."

"No," Laura said. "He didn't rape me. That's not what this guy wanted."

"Okay. What *did* he want?"

Laura finished the last of her beer. Then, she crushed the can and tossed it at her feet. "When I was out of it, he put me on the bed and filmed me in all sorts of compromising positions. Made it look like–"

She took a deep breath.

"This guy, he was doing all kinds of terrible things. At the same time, nothing happened. But it looked bad. Looked like he was doing all kinds of perverted shit, putting bottles inside me. Using sex toys. And the way he edited the footage–"

"Made it look like you were enjoying it," Roz said.

"Yep."

"What did he want?"

"He wanted a favour," Laura said, hugging her knees and pulling them in tight. "I was lot prettier back then. Conventionally pretty, as they say. I took care of myself. He wanted to use that to make his wife jealous. She'd left him. He wanted her back. That old story."

"He wanted an ornament?"

"Yep. And if I didn't do what he wanted, he said he'd release the footage to everyone. Friends, family. And of course, Tommy."

"Tommy? The guy you were supposed to marry?"

Laura nodded. "I had no choice, Roz. I was shit-scared. I didn't want that footage getting out and I figured it was a one-time only thing."

"So what happened?"

Laura longed for another beer. But she wanted the open road more. She lit up a cigarette instead, offering one to Roz, who shook her head.

"No thanks, hon."

"Anyway," Laura said, after a deep inhale. "Long story short, it didn't work out. He got mad, blamed it on me and did exactly what he said he was going to do. He put the footage everywhere. And I mean everywhere. He emailed it to Tommy at work, put it on every social media platform going, and even sent it to my parents' private email address. How he got that, I'll never know."

"Motherfucker."

"The footage went viral," Laura said. "That was the day I stopped being a person and became a meme."

Roz squinted. "A what?"

"A meme. A joke on the internet."

"Because of this guy's film?"

"Yes."

"Can't say I fully understand all this internet stuff," Roz said. "But fuck."

Laura smoked like it was a race to lung cancer. "My life was over. And I had a pretty good life too. I had a great job that I loved, a fiancée who adored me, friends and family, a great little dog and a nice flat. I didn't realise how good I had it until it was gone. Until I became the Don't Drink Girl."

"The Don't Drink Girl?"

Laura had to laugh at the look of bewilderment on Roz's

face. "That's who I am now. At least, according to the internet."

"You're the Don't Drink Girl?"

"Yep."

"And what does *she* do?"

"She's a warning. This is what happens to good girls who drink too much."

"Holy shit."

Roz finished her beer, then tossed it into the pile for shooting. She stood up, joints creaking. Stretching to her full height, which from Laura's perspective on the grass, was higher than the sun. "That twisted bastard should be in prison for wrecking your life."

"I tried telling people. No one believed me."

"Think I will have that cigarette."

Roz took a cigarette out of Laura's pack. She lit up and blew a cloud of smoke across the garden. "*No one?* Your own family didn't believe you?"

Laura hesitated. "You haven't seen the footage."

"What about Tommy?"

Laura felt the old knots tighten in her chest. "He was a wreck. It destroyed him. Once he'd seen it, that was it. Oh, it didn't fall apart right away. We carried on for a while. He tried to make it work, but he couldn't get those images out of his head. In the end, he wouldn't touch me. Wouldn't even look at me. And I don't blame him."

"And your parents?"

Laura lit the next cigarette. Her hand trembling as it carried the lighter to the tip.

"Couldn't look me in the eyes."

"I can't imagine."

"My whole world crashed down at breakneck speed. I didn't sleep well for months. I don't sleep that good even now. I cried. I drank. Did all of that. In the end, I wasn't me anymore. Not in the eyes of the people who mattered."

"If it's any consolation," Roz said, "I've never seen a meme or video with your face on it."

"When was the last time *you* were on the internet?"

"Shit. What year was Myspace all the rage?"

They both laughed. Laura stood up, dusting down the back of her jeans. "So, there you go. That's my sad story."

Roz nodded. "Want another beer?"

"Not for me," Laura said. She held the cigarette in her lips. Reached over and grabbed the Remington leaning against the house. Threw the strap over her shoulder.

"One's my limit. I'm going to keep my promise and go down to Skiach. Eat something. Then it's back to work."

"You're not seriously going back on the road, are you?" Roz asked. "Take a few days off. Rest. Do something else besides driving and selling jewellery at the side of the road. Or if you really have to work, make some necklaces."

Laura walked away with a wave. "The tourists are coming. Gotta make the most of busy season, right?"

"Fair enough. What about the materials you wanted?"

"To tell you the truth," Laura said, turning back to Roz. "I've got plenty of stuff in the van. Guess I just needed a chat."

Roz blew her a kiss. "Anytime sweetheart."

Laura waved again. Then set off towards the campervan. Even after a short stop at the farmhouse, she was restless for the road. Craving movement. The anonymity. It was the only comfort left to her.

10

DIRK

"Can you *please* put something else on?" Isla said, both hands clamped over her ears. "I can't listen to that horrible Dad-Rock for one second longer."

"Dad-Rock!"

Diana howled with laughter.

Dirk, sitting in the driver's seat, glanced at his wife beside him. Then, he looked over his shoulder at his stepdaughter, sitting in the back beside her brother. "You're crazy. I'm playing back-to-back classics here young lady. Anyway, I thought you were listening to podcasts."

"Not for the past half hour," Isla said, taking her hands off her ears. "I wish though."

Dirk shrugged, then turned his attention back to the road. What did kids today know about good music? What was wrong with *Ultimate Driving Rock Hits* on shuffle? Better than what this internet-obsessed, mollycoddled generation was coming up with. All their music sounded like a chipmunk singing over a drum machine.

I'm driving, he thought. *My rules.*
My music.

He turned the volume up as Whitesnake's 'Here I Go Again' blasted out of the speakers.

"Dad, please."

"Okay."

He turned it down. Just a little.

Diana gave him a scathing look, then went back to browsing through her well-worn copy of the NC500 guide book.

The family were travelling north in their hired Fiat Ducato. Adults up front, kids sitting behind in a row of seats with a sliding table. Isla had been scrolling through her phone non-stop since leaving Edinburgh, headphones glued to her ears. Joe was playing his PlayStation Portable, ignoring Diana's orders to take regular breaks.

They'd set off early, just after six o'clock. Made good time by avoiding the worst of the morning traffic around Edinburgh. Dirk had driven all the way, despite Diana's regular offers to take over the wheel. Dirk was fine. He didn't need anyone else to drive. They'd passed Inverness and were, at present, on the southern stretch of the NC500. The plan now was to stop at Skiach Services on the way north. Treat themselves to a big breakfast before the holiday activities got underway.

"Are we stopping soon?" Isla asked. "I'm starving."

Diana looked up from the guide book. A glance at her daughter in the back. "Told you to eat some toast this morning, didn't I?"

Isla made a gasping noise. "I wasn't hungry at five o'clock in the morning. Who in their right mind eats food at that time of day?"

"Not long now," Dirk said. "Skiach services coming up soon."

"I'm thinking about taking up the guitar," Joe said. The boy's voice came out of nowhere. First time he'd looked up from his PlayStation Portable in an hour. First time he'd spoken in more than two.

Isla sniggered.

Diana groaned. Lowered her book again. She looked at her son like he'd just come out as a Satan worshipper. "What?"

"I wanna play the guitar."

"Where'd that come from, champ?" Dirk asked. He wondered if it was the endless stream of classic rock that had inspired the boy's decision.

"Been thinking about it for a while."

"First I've heard of it," Diana said.

Isla's face was a mask of contempt. "The guitar? *You?* You think that actually playing the guitar, a *real* guitar, is the same thing as playing *Guitar Hero*?"

Joe was calm. "No, I don't."

"Yes, you do."

"Mind your own business."

"Joe, there are hamsters out there who've got a better chance of playing the guitar than you do."

Joe's sense of calm was short-lived.

"I said, shut up!"

He whacked his sister on the arm. A low thudding noise that made Dirk wince. They'd done well up until now. No squabbling or sibling-to-sibling violence until the Highlands, something to be grateful for at least.

"I'll remind you of what you said a year from now," Joe said. "When I'm an expert. When I can play *anything*."

"Do that, rock star."

Diana braved a smile as she looked at Dirk. "Kids are hungry."

Dirk nodded. "Like I said, we're nearly there. Skiach coming up soon, guys."

Husband and wife exchanged glances. In the week leading up to their departure, Dirk and Diana had discussed their mutual concern about how Isla would cope with two weeks in the campervan, especially with Joe. The kids got on each other's nerves at the best of times. The Ducato was a big enough campervan, but it was going to be a challenge, the four of them living on top of one another. That didn't happen at home. There were bedrooms to go to. Here, there was nothing. Zero personal space, besides going to the bathroom. The sleeping arrangements consisted of two sets of bunk beds at the back. The beds were jammed tight together. Not ideal for any of them, but especially Isla, who was at a sensitive age. She'd made it clear from the start that a family road trip held little appeal, but Diana insisted. The NC500 was Diana's dream. She wanted her daughter there.

Joe put his PlayStation on the table. "Where's the nearest music shop?"

Dirk glanced out the side window. There was little traffic around and it felt like they had the Highland scenery to themselves.

"Inverness, I suppose."

"That's back the way, isn't it?"

"Sure is," Dirk said.

"Can we stop in there on the way back to Edinburgh? Have a look at the guitars?"

Diana snapped the book shut. Sounded like a whip cracking in Dirk's head. She placed it on her lap, then let out a long sigh. "Joe. We're not getting you a guitar. You'll be obsessed for a while, sure. You'll play it for about a week, get frustrated, and then it'll be another thing clogging up space in your room."

"It won't."

"Wouldn't be the worst thing in the world," Dirk said. "Learning how to play a musical instrument. Wish I'd done it at his age."

Joe pumped a fist in the air. "Yes."

Diana glared at her husband. "Thanks for the support, good cop."

Dirk mouthed the word 'sorry' to his wife. Just then, the sign for Skiach Services appeared up ahead, like a mirage at the side of the road. Half a mile away.

"Thank God," Isla said.

Dirk drummed his fingers off the steering wheel. Two weeks of bliss. He couldn't wait to make memories. He even started whistling a little Whitesnake, just for Isla's benefit.

11

DIRK

"Here we go," Dirk said, manoeuvring the Ducato into a vacant parking spot.

It was his first time parking the campervan, the biggest thing he'd ever driven. It went well. No hiccups. He slotted the vehicle into a space across from the front of the services. *Good job*, he thought, congratulating himself. His driving skills weren't rusty. Not that he missed driving as a full-time job. Working with Diana's dad, Jack, was a pleasure. He loved the furniture store. Loved the customers. And to top it off, Dirk was a better salesman than he thought.

He turned off the engine. Lifted the handbrake.

"Everybody out," Diana said. She slipped her guide book into the side pocket. Found a space amongst all the food wrappers and a banana peel.

The kids didn't need to be told twice.

Joe pulled the side door open. Both he and Isla leapt out of the van like it was about to explode in a ball of flames. Diana followed her children outside, standing by the passenger side door, stretching her arms above her head to get the blood flowing. After a moment, she looked towards the main building. Dirk noticed her expression darkening. Then, she cupped her hands over her mouth, yelling at the kids to slow down.

Dirk glanced to his right.

The kids were sprinting across the car park towards the front door.

Diana yelled for a second time, repeating the command to slow down. Dirk didn't like the shrill tone in his wife's voice. She was really scared.

"Idiots," he said.

He pulled the keys out of the ignition and jumped outside. Legs stiff. Back, a little tight. That's when he saw Isla and Joe running straight into the path of a red and white campervan that was making its way around the car park.

Diana's body visibly shuddered. She let out a wild shriek.

"Oh my God!"

The campervan screeched to a halt. Inches from Isla and Joe. The kids stood on the road, frozen like two rabbits caught in the headlights.

Dirk stared at the van in horror. Surely, a shouting match was inevitable. He waited for the driver to throw the door open and charge out, ranting and raving. They had every right to be furious. The kids had messed up. Which meant that as parents, he and Diana had messed up by letting them run off like that.

Shit, he thought.

Was he about to get into a fight with another campervan driver?

On the first day, of all days.

The other van was a Volkswagen Grand California.

Lovely red and white finish. Dirk recognised it because he'd considered renting that same model for the trip, instead of the Ducato. In the end, a better price and more convenient pickup location was the difference between the two models.

The California remained in the middle of the road. The engine ticked over, smoke blowing out of the exhaust. Time stopped. All the other people in the car park faded into the background. Grey silhouettes, a world apart from the unfolding drama. Isla and Joe, after nearly getting killed, ran off without signalling an apology to whoever was behind the wheel. They crossed the road and disappeared through the sliding doors.

Dirk felt like his feet were glued to the asphalt.

Diana appeared at his side. Face bright red, eyes wide. Out of breath. "Did you see that? They didn't even look where they were going. Morons!"

Dirk took her hand. Locked fingers together.

"They're okay."

He squeezed.

"C'mon," he said. "We'd better get in there before they get us in even more trouble."

They walked hand-in-hand, slowing down a beat as they approached the Grand California. It was still there, directly in front of the building. Engine running. Looked like whoever was behind the wheel was waiting.

Dirk felt a sudden cold sensation. As he walked past the van, he couldn't bring himself to look at the driver's face. Couldn't bring himself to signal an apology. What good would it do? And besides, the driver didn't know that Joe and Isla were his kids.

It was Diana who waved to the driver.

"I think it's a woman behind the wheel."

Dirk kept his eyes on the sliding doors. "Oh."

That was something. At least it wasn't a man driving the Grand California. Less chance of him getting beat up and humiliated in front of his wife.

Only when he reached the doors, did Dirk turn around again. He even lifted his hand to wave. Why not?

But the campervan had moved on.

12

LAURA

Laura couldn't find a parking space.

There were more people at the services this morning than she'd expected. More cars coming in and out. Early start. Tourists everywhere. This was the summer rhythm and it was only just getting started for the year. Not that she was complaining. Best time of year for selling.

Still, some of the tourists couldn't park their rentals for shit. Like, why was that Astra taking up two parking spaces? Laura cursed the driver, steered the California away, prepping for a second lap. She sped up. That's when she almost hit two kids who ran out onto the road. Laura slammed the brakes. There was a loud screech that raked the inside of her head.

"Fuck."

The kids stood there, vacant-eyed. Then, they ran off without apologising. Two little bastards who'd almost given her a heart attack, disappearing through the sliding doors.

Laura watched them go. Then she closed her eyes. Took five deep breaths before driving on.

The near miss wasn't her fault, but still. No more beers in the morning. Not if she was driving.

Eventually, she found a vacant spot. Laura parked up, then walked towards the front door, hands shoved deep in her pockets. It was still cold, but the weather forecast said to expect a pleasant eighteen degrees Celsius by twelve o'clock.

Her phone vibrated in her pocket.

Laura tensed up. There'd been another missed call on the drive to Skiach. That was two now from her parents in Glasgow and it was still early in the day.

What did they want?

Should she just turn the damn phone off? Not like she used it much.

Laura's only plan for the rest of the day was to lose herself in work. Start off with a light breakfast here at the services, then drive north and pitch up for the morning. She wanted the sun shining on her face. After that, all she could do was wait for the tourists to start showing up. If she had a *really* good day, she'd finish early and start working on new stock. She had some good ideas up her sleeve – a new range of summer-themed bracelets that she'd been planning since last year. Working in the van wasn't ideal, both for space and tidiness reasons. It looked like a bomb had gone off in the back. The cotton twine, beads, needles, copper pipe and all the rest of it was lying around everywhere. Zero organisation. These items, what was left of them, were the mementos that Laura had taken from Masons on her last day in the studio. Walking out the front door that day, fighting back the tears, a big cardboard box in her arms. The last time. Her heart breaking. A box full of tools, materials and some of the creative pieces she'd made. Those pieces would only end up in the bin if left behind. And Laura worked too hard to let that happen. So yeah, she took it all and became something of a hoarder. The back of the van was a state, but so what? Nobody saw it but her.

Laura reached the sliding doors. They opened as a sixty-something man, with a Rangers cap on his head, was coming out. He smiled. Deep laughter lines formed in the corners of his eyes.

"Good morning," he said, his voice a cheery lilt.

"Morning."

Laura's reply was gruff. She hurried past the man before any other remarks or attempt to further the conversation. Her heart raced. Here she was again, trapped indoors with all these strangers. Why did she do this to herself? Surrounding herself with people hadn't been comfortable in five years. Not like it used to be. How many of them knew about the Don't Drink Girl? She played the emergency broadcast in her mind. The rational voice inside Laura, soft and calming, went through the old routine, reminding her that there was little chance of anyone recognising her. Her hair was short. Dyed blue. Still, the fear was there. It always flared up when she was at close quarters with so many people. Her face (as well as other parts of her body) had been seen by almost everyone with an internet connection.

She entered the crowded restaurant area – a large room with wooden floors and large windows that gorged on the morning sunlight. Tall wooden tables, scattered everywhere. The drone of morning chatter. Knives and forks scraping off plates.

Breathe, she told herself. *You can do this.*

Head down, she walked to the counter. Lifted a tray off the rack, shuffled forward with everyone else in the queue.

Feeling eyes on her at all times, even if no one was looking. She grabbed a bottle of orange juice, a banana and some yoghurt. Dumped then on the tray. Maybe she'd have toast and coffee too. Most days, Laura forgot to eat until the light-headedness reminded her. Food, like so many other things, just didn't seem that important anymore.

She glanced over her shoulder. Any tables? The endless sea of faces, all blurring into one, made her dizzy. *Abandon the tray*, she urged herself. *Go to the newsagent at the front door, buy a sandwich and get the hell out of here.*

No.

She persevered with her search for a seat. There had to be at least one table where she could sit–

Laura felt like she'd been punched in the stomach.

She fell back against the counter.

"What the–?"

The realisation of what she was looking at, of *who* she was looking at, slowly began to sink in. It was like being squeezed in a vice, all the air wrung out of her.

She blinked hard.

Would he disappear?

He didn't. She checked the other tables to see if he was sitting there too. Trying to figure out if all this was a cruel trick of the mind. A figment of her imagination. He'd haunted her nightmares for this long, hadn't he?

Nope.

It was him. It was Dirk. And he was sitting at *that* table.

Laura felt lightheaded. She turned back to the counter, feeling the walls close in all around her. She had to get her shit together. Process. She focused on her breath. It took about a minute, but the dizziness slowly began to pass. It was as if her body had rebooted after a sudden systems error.

She moved in time with the queue. With the other diners, but a world away. She worked her way slowly to the woman at the checkout.

Another look over her shoulder.

She felt the blood whooshing in her veins.

He wasn't alone. There was a woman and two children with him. All acting very familiar with one another. Was that *his* family? The woman wasn't Court. And the kids were a little too young to be his biological children, the ones he'd told her about in Glasgow. Did the bastard have a new family?

Laura couldn't take her eyes off him. Dirk looked *well*. He wasn't dead in the eyes like he'd been back then. He'd lost a little weight and there was a flush of colour in his cheeks. This wasn't the dour, grey-faced man that Laura remembered from back then. There was *life* in this man. The difference between now and then was striking.

How was that fair?

She turned back to the counter, heart thumping.

Shouldn't he be dead? Suicide felt like the natural progression, considering the dark hole he'd fallen into back then. Bottle of pills. Rope. Knife to the wrist. His bloated, stinking corpse discovered in a cheap hotel room (maybe that *same* hotel room) after another guest complained about the smell.

That was still better than what he deserved. A hell of a lot less than what he'd done to her.

Deep down, Laura had always hoped he was alive. Miserable. Rotting in his skin. Suffering in excruciating pain or living with a degenerative illness that slowly sucked the life out of him. Maybe he was in jail. Maybe he had brain damage. There had to be some sort of accountability for his wicked deeds.

And now, *this*?

He was alive. Better than alive. He was happy, talking to his wife and children and shovelling a thick slice of toast and jam into his mouth. Like he hadn't seen food in weeks. Anyone looking at Dirk over there wouldn't see anything out of the ordinary. They'd see the most normal guy in the world. Good guy. Good husband. Good old Dad.

Laura knew exactly what he was. A monster in the everyman's clothing.

It was as if talking about him with Roz, finally opening up as she'd done that morning, had summoned him to Laura. A gift from the universe?

She closed her eyes. There it was. The smell of his cigarette smoke drifting up her nostrils. She was back in the filthy hotel, sitting up in bed with a splitting headache, covering herself with paper-thin sheets. Listening to Dirk as he outlined the blackmail scheme.

A faint voice behind her.

"Excuse me."

Laura ignored it. She could hear Tommy crying in the bedroom at their flat in Hyndland. Door closed. Tommy and Freddie in there, Laura locked out. The realisation that she wasn't getting married. That she wasn't with him anymore. She could see the disgust and disappointment in her parents' eyes. Looking at her like she was a stranger. A slut. A disgrace. And once more, that feeling as she walked out of work. Her colleagues pretending not to look. Nobody offering even a crumb of comfort because they thought she'd brought it on herself.

There she goes.

Goodbye, Laura Hansen. Hello, The Don't Drink Girl.

That faint voice behind her was louder.

"Excuse me."

Someone tapped her on the shoulder. Laura flinched. There was a polite smile on the face of the silver-haired woman standing behind her in the queue.

"Are you still in the queue, love?"

Laura apologised. Caught up with the rest of the line. She held the tray ahead of her, arms extended. Feeling stiff from head to toe. Every movement felt awkward.

Take deep breaths, a voice said.

The calming voice belonged to Roz.

The woman sitting beside Dirk was in good shape. Long dark hair tied back into a ponytail. Athletic build, maybe a runner? Didn't look insane or desperate. Clearly, she had no idea what sort of man she was with. He'd conned her.

"Can I help you?" the woman behind the counter asked.

Laura flinched again. She'd reached the end of the line. "Sorry. What?"

The woman looked surprised by the question. She pointed at Laura's tray on the counter. "Just the orange juice, yoghurt and banana today, is it?"

Laura's nod was mechanical. "And a black coffee please."

"Black coffee. That's all?"

"Yes. Make that a large one."

Laura paid in cash.

"Thanks very much," the woman said, handing Laura a few coins in change. Her accent was a friendly, musical lilt that never wavered. "Someone will bring your coffee over in a minute. Have a good day."

Laura managed a weak smile. She walked away, tray in hand. Felt like she was floating across the room.

Did he see me? Has he recognised me?

She had to find a table quick. Fortunately for Laura, an elderly couple were finishing up their breakfast at one of the smaller tables near the exit. They stood up, wiping themselves down for crumbs. Running napkins over their mouths. Laura was all over it. She hurried across the dining room, claiming the space as soon as the old couple shuffled away together. There were dirty cups and plates on the tables. Laura didn't care. She sat down, slid the plates to the other side of the table. She'd found a good spot. One that offered a decent view of Dirk and his family.

She stared at the back of his head. There was an emerging bald spot that hadn't been there five years ago.

"Fuck."

The two kids. The same little shits she'd almost run over in the car park.

Laura sat rigid and upright. Like someone had stuffed a mannequin into one of the chairs. A mannequin with a pounding heart. Why was she so afraid? Even if Dirk did look over his shoulder, what were the chances he'd recognise her? The scruffy clothes, short blue hair and no makeup were her disguise these days. The old Laura Hansen, the pretty little blonde, was no more.

There he was. Within arm's reach. All these years, she'd never dreamed of seeing this man again.

She picked up a knife off the table. Squeezed the handle so hard it felt like something in her arm would snap.

He was a sitting duck.

Laura knew what she had to do.

All of Dirk's newfound happiness, she would take it away. All the joy, all the love that had brought the colour back into his cheeks, she'd squeeze it out of his life. Just like he'd done to her. His people would suffer. Just like her people had suffered.

It was payback time.

She'd kill him.

Today.

13

LAURA

Laura sipped her coffee. Watched the family as they ate breakfast.

She hadn't touched the food on her tray. She hadn't been hungry coming into Skiach and she sure as hell wasn't hungry now.

The dining hall was full of distraction. To Laura, it was one big cacophony of background noise – the sound of people eating breakfast, different accents and languages intermingling over the sound of lukewarm pop music spilling out of the speakers. A lot of the people inside the restaurant would be travelling north on the NC500 later that day. Future customers. These people had money to spend.

Laura didn't give a damn about selling jewellery. Making money was the last thing on her mind today.

She continued to stare at the back of Dirk's head. Watching as he slurped his coffee. As he gorged on a greasy fry-up, his cheeks bulging out in a grotesque circular motion as he chewed his food.

Monster, Laura thought.

Her day was blown wide open. There was no way that Laura could sit at the side of the road, selling bracelets and necklaces to tourists, knowing that Dirk was so close. Knowing that he was happy. Content. Enjoying all the things he'd stolen from her life.

She'd found him.

And she was ready to do this.

Where were they going, this family of four? Were they heading north on the NC500 or coming back down towards Inverness? Were they even on holiday or did they live around here? Surely not. Laura would have seen him before now. Had to be a holiday. A road trip. What sort of vehicle were they travelling in? A car? A campervan?

How was she going to do it?

How was she going to end this man's life?

The girl at Dirk's table stood up. She said something to the woman, then walked away from the others. Laura's eyes followed the movement. She watched the girl, who was tall for her age, glide across the floor. Nice looking kid. Dyed blonde hair, a red and black checked shirt, unbuttoned to reveal a white t-shirt underneath. Her denim shorts were ripped. There was a bored look on her face. But she was elegant and that would shine in the years to come. People would fall in love with her easily.

The thought of a girl like that living with Dirk made Laura uneasy. All the more reason to take him out.

The girl made her way towards the exit, pulling a phone out of her pocket. She kept her head down, thumb sliding up and down the screen. Almost bumped into a family of diners waiting at the counter.

Laura pushed her chair back. She grabbed the orange juice off the table, leaving the food behind. With a final glance at Dirk, she followed the girl out of the dining room, walking into the main entrance area. This part of the building wasn't as sickeningly bright as the interior of the restaurant.

There were still far too many people. Too many for Laura to get comfortable.

She followed the girl to the ladies' room, located next to the sliding doors. Waited outside, pacing back and forth. Realising how strange she must have looked, she forced herself to stand still. Shoved her hands in her pockets. One leg trembled. There it was, that icy cold feeling creeping up her spine. Too many people. Some of them passing by a little too close for comfort. God, she hated living like this. It felt like everyone in the building was staring at her. Like they wanted to approach. To say something.

Hey, you're the girl in all those memes, aren't you? The Don't Drink Girl. Look everyone, here she is, here's the SLUT right–

The bathroom door swung open.

Laura rushed forward, bumping her shoulder into the girl. They collided in the doorway and Laura gasped.

"Oh shit," she said, throwing up her hands. "I'm such an idiot."

She stood in front of the girl, blocking her escape. Kept her voice nice and friendly. Embarrassed smile on her face.

"Sorry about that. Are you okay?"

The girl nodded. She was blushing.

"Yeah."

"Damn," Laura said, hoping the smile on her face wasn't too manic. "Wasn't watching where I was going."

The girl was still nodding. Still blushing.

Laura narrowed her eyes. Took a step backwards. "Hey, you look familiar. Don't I know you from somewhere?"

The girl frowned, but she was blushing harder. "Umm...no."

"Oh, I think so. We kind of met already. You're the one I almost ran over in the car park about a half-hour ago. You and the boy. Your brother, is he?"

The girl looked at the floor. There was an embarrassed smile on her face and she couldn't look Laura in the eye.

"Sorry."

Laura shrugged. "Hey, don't worry about it. No harm done. Not this time at least." She jerked a thumb over her shoulder. "Saw you in the restaurant back there. Are you on holiday with your family?"

"Ummm, yeah. Road trip."

"You don't sound too excited. Not much fun trailing around with your folks and little brother twenty-four seven, is it?"

The girl's eyes lit up. Like she saw a kindred spirit in front of her. At that moment, her rigid shoulders visibly relaxed. "No."

"Well," Laura said, her eyes skimming the surroundings. Checking for any of the girl's family members who might be looking for her. "This might sound weird. But enjoy it while you can. It sucks, I know, but we don't have our families around forever. I wish I could do a road trip with my parents. Know what I mean?"

"Uh-huh."

"Heading up the NC500?"

"Yep."

Laura made a soft whistling noise. "Good times. That's a beautiful route, take it from me. I work that route most days, selling handcrafted jewellery and I'm telling you, it's some of the best scenery you'll ever see."

The girl's expression was polite, but confused.

"You guys got a campervan?" Laura asked, taking a step closer. She was still directly in front of the girl. Blocking the exit.

"We rented one."

"Cool. What did you get?"

"I can't remember the name of it."

Laura nodded. She realised she was staring too hard. Her smile felt like a grimace. At the same time, she tried to remind herself that this girl had nothing to do with Dirk's crime. God knows, she might even be a victim herself. She was pretty, but awkward. Tall and gangly, not quite at home in her own skin yet.

"What's your name?"

"Isla."

"That's a nice name."

"Thanks."

"So, you're travelling with your mum and dad?"

"Well, he's actually my stepdad."

"Right. Where you heading next? North or south?"

"North," the girl said. "This is our first day on the road."

Their first day.

Laura felt a rush of excitement. It was like a switch turning on inside her. The electricity soaring through her bloodstream. She backed off, allowing the girl room to pass. "Well, I hope you guys have a great trip."

"Thanks," Isla mumbled.

Laura walked past her, pushing the bathroom door open. She went inside. The bathroom was tiny and it reeked of strong air freshener. Lemon and lime. Laura was greeted by the sound of a blaring hand dryer.

She hurried inside one of the cubicles. Locked the door,

then sat down on the toilet. Her heart was thumping. There was every chance that she might have to throw up before going back outside. Still, it had been a success. She got the information she wanted. The family's NC500 trip was just beginning. It was day one. They were heading north.

And so was she.

14

LAURA

Laura's tar-stained fingers drummed the steering wheel. She hummed a tune. Something that she'd heard on the radio that morning on her way down to Skiach. Couldn't remember what it was called. Or who sung it. She always hummed when she was nervous. One of many little quirks that went back to childhood.

They'd be coming out soon.

Any minute now.

What was taking them so long?

Her back was pressed tight against the driver's seat. Eyes glued to the side mirror, watching people go in and out through the sliding doors. She was afraid to blink. As she waited for him to come out, Laura was still trying to process what just happened in the restaurant. Seeing Dirk after all these years. Seeing a happy, contented version of Dirk with a nice family. Living the good life. What the fuck?

Even now, her hands wouldn't stop shaking.

She blinked hard, moisturising her eyes. Returned her focus to the side mirror.

"C'mon."

Sitting there with nothing to do but think, it was all coming back to her. Like it had just happened again. She'd relived that feeling a thousand times. How many nights had she lain awake in bed, thinking about the life she'd lost? Her career. Marrying Tommy. Travelling. Working overseas. Children, never a certainty but a possibility. There were so many things she could've done. Before he closed the doors out of spite.

There was no way of getting it back. All that was gone forever. But Dirk was here. And she had the chance to take his happiness away.

An eye for an eye.

Laura checked the knife she kept strapped with tape under the passenger seat. For safety reasons. Same reason she had a gun. She ran her fingers over the titanium handle. She kept the knife sharp on a sanding block. There was another knife in the bedroom, a smaller one, but no less sharp.

Her eyes returned to the mirror.

Where was that bastard?

The plan, as much as Laura had formulated one, was simple. Follow Dirk's campervan north. Didn't matter where they were going. Laura had almost a full tank of petrol. The Grand California would shadow Dirk for as long as it had to. Stop when he stopped. Follow him on foot and wait for the right opportunity to present itself. And it would present itself, sooner or later.

Laura sat bolt upright.

They were coming out. One big happy family coming through the sliding doors. Dirk leading the way, his wife and the two kids trailing behind them as they walked across the car park.

Laura felt a rush of blood to the head. *Deep breaths.*

She turned the key in the ignition and the California shuddered as it woke up. She sat still, waiting for the family to get into their vehicle. They stopped at a Ducato parked on the other side of the car park.

Nice van, Laura thought.

The woman walked around to the driver's side. Opened the van up. Dirk hopped into the passenger seat while the kids jumped in the back, sliding the door shut behind them. The campervan backed out of the parking spot, then crawled towards the exit.

The adrenaline coursed through Laura's veins. She reversed the California out of its space. Almost slammed into the side of an incoming Tesla. The driver blared the horn. Yelled something in a language she didn't understand.

Fuck, she thought.

Laura drove the California towards the exit. Fighting back the urge to be sick.

"Calm down," she said. "Breathe. In for four, hold, out for four, hold. Breathe for God's sake."

She felt better on the open road. This was home. This was her world and the thing she knew best of all nowadays. Pressing the accelerator to the floor, the Grand California caught up with the Ducato in no time.

"I found you," she whispered.

Didn't matter where the road took them. Dirk was a man swimming in shark-infested waters.

He was as good as dead.

15

DIRK

"The Fyrish Monument," Dirk said, reading aloud from Diana's guide book. "That's where we're going next."

His eyes skimmed the pictures and text. Recalling the time Diana had told him about the monument and how they should include it on the trip.

"This'll be our first proper stop on the NC500."

"I hope everyone's excited," Diana said, taking a left, steering the van onto the B9176. It was still early and the B-road was quiet.

Isla made a long, drawn-out groaning noise from the back. It was a noise she was particularly good at. "Fyrish Monument? What's that? A statue or something?"

"It's not a statue," Dirk said. "You'll see for yourself when you get up there. Think of it as a chance to walk off breakfast."

"Walk?" Joe said, sounding alarmed.

Dirk browsed through the guide book. "Don't panic.

You're not climbing Mount Everest. It'll be good for you. For all of us."

Diana glanced in the side mirror. "Looks like we're not the only ones getting an early start. There's one campervan behind us. I think it's a safe bet they're heading to the monument too."

"That's a Grand California," Dirk said, looking in the passenger side mirror. He leaned forward for a better look. "Uh-oh. Looks like the same Grand California that almost hit Joe and Isla in the car park."

"You're kidding?"

"Nope. Same colours."

Diana winked at Dirk. "Maybe they want to finish what they started."

"Maybe," Dirk said, "it's a Terminator campervan."

"Not funny," Isla said from the back.

Five minutes later, they arrived in the small purpose-built car park that was the starting point for the monument. To Dirk's surprise, there weren't many spaces left. He was glad that he'd suggested the early start out of Edinburgh. Turned out his obsessive planning had its uses after all. Not that he was one to gloat.

Diana carefully inserted the Ducato into a vacant parking spot. She switched off the engine and everyone got out. Diana and the kids grabbed their walking boots out the back, then leaned up against the van while they switched footwear. Dirk, already wearing his brand-new Caterpillars, watched the red and white Grand California turn into the car park. The campervan glided past them. There was a woman behind the wheel. Blue hair. Pale skin. She didn't look at the family as she drove past.

He laughed to himself.

It was only a woman. Nothing to feel uneasy about.

The California continued towards the opposite end of the parking area. The driver tucked the van neatly into the second-to-last space.

He glanced at his family. They were still putting on their shoes. Going a bit too slow, looked like they needed some motivation.

Dirk clapped his hands together.

"C'mon. We've still got a lot to do today."

Isla was complaining to anyone who'd listen that her boots weren't comfortable. She walked a few steps across the car park and winced. Looked like she was trying to win an Oscar for her performance.

"Feels like they're eating my feet!"

"You tried them on in the shop," Diana said, catching up with Dirk. She threaded her arm through his. "You said they were fine."

"Yeah, but they hurt now."

Diana beckoned her kids to follow the adults. Her face creasing up with impatience. "Oh my God. You just need some time to break them in. Stop complaining about everything Isla and start walking. Besides, it's not that far to the top."

Dirk paid no attention to the family skirmish. With a spring in his step, he led the others to the start of the walking trail that wound its way uphill to the Fyrish Monument. There was a feeling of absolute contentment that he wanted to cling to forever. The sun was out. The sky was clear and the birds were singing.

What a day to be alive, he thought.

They trekked up the 'Jubilee Path'. Dirk led with an enthusiastic stride, listening as Diana, bringing up the rear, shared snippets of information about the monument with Isla and Joe. Clearly, she'd picked up a lot from the guide book. She explained, in the voice of a seasoned tour guide, how Fyrish was an eighteenth-century trio of arches flanked by a set of stone pillars. It was, she told her less than enthusiastic audience, designed to honour the gates on the city wall of Negapatam in India.

"Nega-what?" Joe asked, breathing hard.

The ascent meandered through a stretch of pine forest. It took about forty minutes in total to go through the woodland and to cross a burn along the way. But as the family approached the summit, they (and all the other tourists) were rewarded with breathtaking views, including the Cromarty Firth and the Black Isle. This, Dirk thought, was the picture postcard version of Scotland, the one that tourists from all over the world flocked to see in their millions every year.

He inhaled the glorious fresh air. Wanted to remember this. Wanted to remember everything about it.

The final section of the hike offered the family a stunning finale as the Fyrish Monument came into view.

"Oh wow," Dirk said, quickening the pace.

His body was nice and loose after the walk, no aches and pains. He pointed at the monument in the distance. "Look at that everyone. See it?"

Diana was a few steps behind him. "Oh my God. It's stunning."

The monument was a huge structure of three central arches and four flanking towers. An impressive, if somewhat strange thing to see at the top of a random hill in the Scottish Highlands. The views were just as impressive, if not more so, than the monument itself. Even the kids, as they caught up with their parents, made oohing noises that at least hinted of excitement.

"Feel free to explore," Dirk said to Isla and Joe. "There's no hurry to go back down."

The kids set off, splitting up within seconds. Dirk and Diana walked in the opposite direction, wandering amongst the other tourists. Dirk locked his arm around Diana's shoulder. He looked back. Isla was already checking her phone, although she'd be lucky to get a signal up here. Joe trudged back and forth, hands in his pockets, staring at the arches. Probably thinking about guitars.

"I'm proud of them," Diana said, nodding at the kids. "Not a word of complaint walking up that hill. And it was steep too."

Dirk smiled. "There's hope."

"That means there's hope for this holiday. I thought for a while there that Isla was going to kick off."

Dirk laughed. "I think they're starting to enjoy themselves."

"Think so?"

"I hope so," Dirk said. "I want this trip to be special for everyone. You most of all. This is your dream."

Diana leaned her head on Dirk's shoulder. She sighed. "I love you."

"Love you too."

Dirk felt the warmth of his wife's body pressed against his. He kissed the top of her head. She looked up at him and they stared into one another's eyes like lovestruck teenagers. For a moment, nothing else existed.

"We're lucky, aren't we?" Diana said, staring at the magnificent view that stretched on for miles.

"I'm the luckiest man in the world."

She nudged him with her elbow. "You're a good man, Dirk de Vries. You deserve to be happy."

He hesitated.

"Do I?"

"We both do."

Dirk held on to her tight. The wind blew in his face. His legs were still warm, a slight twinge in the knees making itself known. There was a slight sensation of floating as he stood there at the top of the hill beside his wife.

Diana lifted her head off his shoulder. Gave him a peck on the cheek.

"I'm going to check on the kids."

"Okay. I'll be around."

Another kiss. Then she set off, walking back towards the central trio of arches.

Dirk wiped the sweat off his brow. He lowered the zip on his North Face jacket, took a step back and stared up at the giant monument. The arches looked like a collection of stone giants, joining hands, raising them aloft. Bizarre but beautiful. He glanced to his right and saw that Diana had already caught up with Isla. Isla was shoving her phone back into her pocket like she'd been busted.

Dirk watched them. Then, his ears pricked up. It was like a primal alarm ringing in his head. Something had disturbed his peace.

Were those footsteps behind him?

He turned around, his blood running cold. As he did, an older man in his fifties, dressed in a khaki shirt, walked past. He greeted Dirk with a smile.

Dirk sighed with relief. His eyes followed the man for a few seconds.

That's when he saw her.

The blue-haired woman was looking directly at him. About ten metres away, close to where the hiking path merged with the summit of the hill. The woman didn't flinch when he looked back at her. There it was, that icy feeling in his veins again. What was she looking at? What did she want? There was a black rucksack draped over her shoulder. He watched as she began to lower the strap, letting it slide over her arm. The bag fell at her feet.

She knelt down, moving her hand towards the zip.

Weirdo, Dirk thought, turning back to the monument.

Just another weirdo.

16

LAURA

Laura's body froze. In a split second, everything stopped working.

It happened just as she reached into the rucksack for the knife. Her body tensed up and she felt like a wishbone about to snap.

Her fingers gripped the knife handle. But she couldn't pull it out. It was like a sudden paralysis at the worst possible moment. He was right there – the man who ruined her life. Right there, waiting for Judgement Day. A few more steps, pull the blade out and plunge it into Dirk's back. Spin him around. Look into his eyes. The last thing he'd hear, apart from the sound of his dying breath, would be Laura's name in his ear.

He'd looked right at her. Then he turned around again, thinking she was just another tourist. A blue-haired nobody.

He doesn't recognise me, Laura thought. *What he did back then. It meant so little to him.*

She'd followed the family to the top of the hill, keeping a

close distance. The track to the monument was one she'd taken several times over the years. Mostly for the solitude she'd experienced at the top, far away from everything and everyone. The best time to come up was late in the day, preferably in winter, when there were no tourists. Wrap up well. Bring a torch. It was quite something.

Laura had to move. She couldn't just stand there like an idiot, her hand stuck in the rucksack. Body and mind out of sync. She had to bring all that hate back to the surface. That would do it. That would get things moving again. Let the hatred bubble up and spill over.

And yet looking at Dirk, Laura felt like a victim again. Naked and humiliated. Hiding behind the sheets. Trapped in a hotel room.

Here was a chance to settle the score. In the nightmares that had plagued her over the past five years, the stranger in that hotel room would sometimes take the shape of a red-skinned devil with sharp horns or some other kind of grotesque monster. His shirt unbuttoned. Smoking. Drinking from a silver flask. This was the same monster who lived rent-free in her mind and there was nothing she could do to evict him.

Until now.

This was her chance. And she couldn't do it. She couldn't do anything. Her hand was still trapped inside the bag, like a foot stuck in the mud.

Laura could feel the sweat running down her face. *Now*, she screamed to herself. *Do it now.* How long could she just stand there, stooped over, hand in the bag, before someone noticed?

How long before they came over? Before they realised that she was trying to pull out a knife?

Laura glanced at Dirk.

He wasn't paying any attention to her. Instead, he was admiring the view. Looking up at the monument and its central arches. Throwing the occasional glance to the right, looking for his family. His contentment was repulsive to Laura. He was so at ease with himself, despite all the things he'd done.

What would Dirk see if he turned around? A madwoman wrestling with something in her rucksack. Nothing more. But he *would* turn around sooner or later and Laura would lose the element of surprise.

Please, she thought. *Let me do this.*

Her arm shot out of the rucksack. No knife. She'd left it in there. *Fuck.* The sweat continued to drip down Laura's face. She stumbled backwards. Away from Dirk. Back onto the path, pushing her way past groups of tourists venturing uphill. All Laura saw was a blur of faces, every one looking at her as if she was crazy.

I'm running away, she thought.

Laura pulled at the zip, closing the rucksack pocket to make sure the knife didn't spill out onto the path. She raced downhill, not stopping to catch breath. She could feel the shame rising up inside her. Chasing her back to the car park.

Coward. She was a coward.

The monster would still be in her dreams.

She barrelled forwards. There were several collisions with tourists. Laura apologised, but she kept going, a runaway boulder slamming into bodies like they were skittles in a bowling alley.

"Excuse me!"

She ran through the pines, cleared the exit and hurried out into the car park. Laura let out a loud gasp. Her lungs were on fire, but there was still no slowing down. She hurried to the Grand California, wrestled with the driver's side door, jumped in and slammed the door shut.

She threw her bag down on the passenger seat.

"FUCK!"

Laura pounded her fists off the the steering wheel.

"FUCK! FUCK! FUCK!"

She grabbed the water bottle out of her bag. Yanked the lid off. Poured it down, spilling most of the liquid down the front of her shirt. She gasped for air. Pulled at the damp shirt, trying to let some cool air in.

It felt like she was on fire.

"I can't do it."

Laura was shaking. The sort of shaking that felt danger-ous. A prelude to disaster. Like she'd just climbed out of icy cold Arctic waters and was minutes away from freezing to death. She focused on her breath, just like Roz had taught her to do when she was stressed. She stared through the windshield, looking at the empty road. Longing for it. And she *could* go if she wanted. The urge to drive away, to disap-pear for a week or two, was overwhelming. *Forget this*, she thought. *Forget all about Dirk*. Go to the far north, find some-where with no people, build a fire and sleep under the stars. Cry. Scream. Heal. She could do whatever she wanted. There was no obligation to commit murder. Laura knew plenty of suitable places. Places that were good for disap-pearing.

"No," she said.

There was no hiding.

Not from herself.

Seeing Dirk had changed everything. She couldn't let him be happy, not after what he did to her. How could she live with that? He took everything. She *had* to kill him. Had to make him suffer, make his people suffer. It was the natural order of things. Eye for an eye. Fuck him and fuck his family. But Laura had just blown the best chance she'd ever get to do it. He'd been inches away from her and she'd choked. Everything, mind and body, had just clammed up.

"Shit."

She looked towards the open road. Heard its call.

So tempting.

Was she really just going to drive off into the sunset? Let that creep go back to living his happy life? And while she lived alone out of a campervan, sleeping on a crummy mattress, reaching a hand out for Tommy in the middle of the night and, instead of his warmth, finding a cold nothing.

Could she just leave it there?

Laura's thoughts were interrupted by her mobile phone ringing. She fished it out of her rucksack. Looked at the screen and grimaced. She waited for her parents to give up, then scrolled to her contacts. She found what she was looking for, hit the call button and put the phone to her ear.

A click.

"Hello darling," said a woman's voice.

"Roz. Thank God."

"What's up darling? Are you out of breath?"

"Roz–"

"What is it?"

Laura's voice trembled as she spoke. With her free hand, she gripped the steering wheel. Held on for dear life.

"Roz, I saw him. He's here."

"You've seen *who*?"

"Dirk De Vries. The guy I told you about this morning. The one who–"

Roz gasped. "Are you kidding me? The one who turned you into a...what did you call it? A meme?"

"He's here. He's fucking here, Roz."

"Oh shit. Are you okay?"

Laura leaned back in the driver's seat. Her body was soaked with sweat. She closed her eyes, reliving events at the top of the hill. What a calamitous fuck up. She reimagined the outcome. This time she didn't freeze. She put the knife in Dirk's heart, his eyes wide with terror as he bled out. At the end, a flicker of recognition as he faced his killer.

"I saw him at Skiach," she said. "After that, I followed him to the Fyrish Monument. He's here, Roz. He's got a wife and two stepchildren. That's his reward for what he did to me. He gets to have all the things he wanted. How's that for fair?"

"And you're sure it's him?"

"It's him."

"Where is he now?"

Laura was lightheaded. She took another sip of water. Worked on her breath, waiting for the fog to clear upstairs. "Still up on the hill, I suppose. Or making his way down."

"Where are you?"

"Car park. Sitting in the van."

"Okay," Roz said. "Sounds like a golden opportunity for payback, hon. What are you going to do about it?"

Laura shook her head. "I had a chance, Roz. I had a chance and–"

Roz cut in. "Not so easy, is it?"

"I blew it."

Laura felt overwhelmed. Exhaustion pressing down on her. The adrenaline dump was well and truly over, and all she wanted to do was crawl into bed, throw the sheets over her head and sleep for a week.

"I don't know if I have it in me."

"It's either that or you drive off," Roz said. "Leave him

alone and let him enjoy his holiday. Does that sit okay with you?"

"No."

"Good."

"But Roz, I froze. I just–"

"I hear you sweetie," Roz said. Her voice was soft and comforting. Sounded like she was talking to a child who thought there was a monster under the bed. "And it's okay, just think of what happened as a dress rehearsal, right? This isn't the end and what's more, you won't be alone next time."

"What do you mean?"

"You're in the car park? At Fyrish?"

"Yes."

Laura heard a noise on the other end of the line, like thudding footsteps. A thump. The loud whack of a door slamming shut. More footsteps, along with the jingle-jangle of keys.

"Roz?" Laura said. "What's going on?"

"Stay where you are," Roz said. "I'm on my way."

17

DIRK

Dirk strolled through the pines, leading his family back out into the car park.

"Well," he said, to Diana and the kids trailing behind him. "Was that fun or was that fun?"

No one answered in words, but Dirk saw that they were smiling. That meant they were as happy as he was. He swung his arms at the side, marching like an overzealous Cub Scout leader, the others lagging behind him as they made their way back to the Ducato.

I feel great, he thought.

The fresh air, exercise and jaw-dropping scenery had revived him after the long drive north from Edinburgh. Dirk was ready for anything. The morning sun kissed his face. His knees were good, having held up well on the descent, despite his fears that the old niggles from his driving years would resurface. But everything was good. He felt like a twenty-year-old again. A man in his prime, with energy for days.

"Watch out for cars," he said to the kids, looking both ways before crossing the car park. He didn't want another repeat of what happened at Skiach.

It was important to set a good example.

He glanced at the Grand California. It was still there, silent at the other end of the car park. Dirk wasn't even sure if it was the same one from Skiach. There were a lot of campervans around this neck of the woods. He didn't remember seeing the blue-haired woman (the weirdo who'd stared at him up on the hill) at Skiach either.

She stood out like a sore thumb.

He'd remember her.

Dirk turned his attention back to his family. Everyone was in good form after the hike, including the kids. There'd been no complaints. No moaning about being bored, tired, too cold, too warm, thirsty or anything else.

Look at them, he thought. They were ready to kill each other on the drive up to Skiach. Now they're walking side by side. Sharing jokes.

There were plenty of reasons to be optimistic about the holiday to come. They had a chance to make precious, life-long memories. Things the kids would look back on fondly in later years. Maybe they'd bring their own kids up here someday. Try to recreate the magic. The road trip had been Diana's dream, but Dirk was heavily invested in its success. He needed this too. There was a clarity of mind in the Highlands that wasn't available in his regular life. Good for reflection. He'd made mistakes. But it was time to forgive himself for the way he'd treated Court and his biological children. He was a different man now. A better man. He wouldn't hurt a fly.

"Not so bad, was it?" Diana asked, as they approached

the van. Her cheeks glowed, complimenting the bright blue of her eyes.

Joe was breathing hard after the downhill jaunt, but he was smiling. "It was fun."

Isla nodded. "Yeah."

"What's next for the gallant adventurers then, hmm?" Dirk asked, doing his best Captain Jack Sparrow impersonation. He stroked his chin, letting the others know he was deep in thought. "Where to mateys? Tain? Portmahomack? Ooh, what if we go to Dornoch and see the Witch's Stone?"

Isla squinted. "The what?"

Diana gave Dirk a lightning-fast peck on the cheek. "Someone's been reading my travel book, eh?"

"I have," Dirk said, putting his arm around his wife's shoulders. There was a massive grin on his face. "And a very interesting book it is too. I can see why you've been glued to it for a month."

"What's the Witch's Stone then?" Isla asked.

Dirk cleared his throat, like he was about to give a speech. "Glad you asked! The Witch's Stone in Dornoch marks the spot where the last witch was executed in Britain. The year was, umm, 1727 or something like that."

"Don't look at me," Diana said. "I didn't memorise dates."

"Why did they execute her?" Isla asked. A question that sounded like an accusation. As if Dirk was somehow involved.

Joe facepalmed. "Duh! Because she was a witch."

"Shut up," Isla snapped.

Diana narrowed her eyes. "Children. You were doing so well."

"Easy now," Dirk said. "It's a good question. Why *did* they execute her? Something about, oh, I can't remember all the details. Didn't she try turning her daughter into a pony? Diana?"

Diana shrugged, content to let Dirk squirm.

"A what?" Joe said, screwing his face up. "A *pony*?"

"Never mind," Diana said. "All will be revealed. So, is that decided? We'll go to Dornoch next?"

"Let's do Tain first," Dirk said. "Then a quick detour to Portmahomack. After that, we'll go up to Dornoch and the caravan park. We have to go to as many places as possible. Cram in as much as we can while we're here, right?"

Diana nodded. She pulled the side door of the campervan open. "How about some tea first? I say we've earned it after that hike."

"Orange juice for me," Isla said, climbing inside the van. She flopped into one of the seats, pulled out her phone and opened up Tik-Tok.

Joe leapt in after his sister. He sat down, grabbing the portable PlayStation off the table. "I'll have some tea and biscuits."

"You know where the biscuits are," Diana said, filling the kettle with water.

Joe grumbled. But he put the PlayStation down, got up and rummaged around the kitchen cupboards until he found the plastic box with the biscuits inside. He grabbed a handful of choc-chip cookies, tossed them onto a plate and took them back to the sliding table.

"This is the life," he said.

That made Diana smile.

Dirk stood at the van door, doing static stretches to avoid stiffening up later around the calves. He watched his family relax inside the van. Kids lost in their gadgets. Diana lining up the mugs, waiting for the kettle to boil. The van was a mess. Spilling over with discarded sweet wrappers, plastic bottles and crisp packets. Dirk felt a jolt of anger. He fought the impulse to start cleaning everything up. Told himself to relax.

You're on holiday.

Then again, it was only day one. Maybe he'd do some cleaning up later. When no one was looking.

18

LAURA

Laura sighed with relief. She watched the white transit van turning off the B-road, pulling into the car park.

"Thank God."

Roz brought the van down the middle of the parking space. There was something predatory about its slow and vigilant crawl. Laura might have imagined it, but it looked like the van stopped for a second right beside Dirk's Ducato. She heard the engine growling. Smoke spitting from the exhaust.

Then it continued towards the Grand California at the back.

Laura drank some water, still trying to rehydrate after running down the hill at breakneck speed. The air conditioning was up full blast, pelting cold air onto her face. Her heart was still racing.

Roz pulled into the space opposite the California. She got out, locked the van and strode across the car park. She was dressed in a scruffy sweater and jeans. A tired pair of black trainers on her feet. Probably no grips left underneath.

There was a large duffel bag on her shoulder.

She walked quickly for such a big woman, as if her presence at the Fyrish Monument was top secret.

"How are you darling?" she said, climbing into the passenger seat. She closed the door and dropped her duffel bag at the footrest. There was a look of concern in her eyes as she studied Laura. "Are you okay?"

Laura nodded. "I feel a lot better now you're here."

"That phone call gave me quite a fright, you know? You sounded a right mess."

"I was."

"But you're okay now?"

"Better at least."

Roz smiled. Then she pointed over Laura's shoulder to the driver's window. "Right, so where is he?"

"See the Ducato over there? It's parked close to the exit."

Laura leaned back, allowing Roz an unobstructed view of the vehicles sitting parallel to the California. The seat groaned under Roz as she came forward. She narrowed her eyes. Nodded. "Yeah, I saw that. Thought he'd be in something like that."

"Looks like he brought the whole family with him," Laura said.

"How many?"

"Three others. A woman and two kids."

"How old are the kids?"

"Early to mid-teens. The boy might even be younger than that."

Roz sighed. "Jeez, that's too bad."

Laura glanced over her shoulder. The side door of Dirk's rental van was partially open, allowing her a view of what was going on inside. Not much, by the looks of it. The two kids were sitting down at a sliding table. Eating, playing on their phones or whatever. The adults were on their feet, tidying up, doing food prep or other chores. It was a nice, relaxed scene. Looked like the family were easing into their holiday.

Laura had to grab the steering wheel. She fought back the urge to scream.

"You alright?" Roz asked.

A weak nod was all Laura could manage. She took her hands off the wheel, leaned back and went back to counting her breath.

"So that's the man who ruined your life?" Roz said, her face a block of unforgiving stone. She was still looking over at the Ducato. Eyes taking it all in. She stroked her chin, deep in thought. "That flimsy-looking piece of shit, eh? Doesn't look like a destroyer of lives from over here, does he?"

"Nope. He's a nice family man now."

"It's always a nice family man."

Roz cut loose with a growl of laughter. She fell back into the seat, pulling a crumpled cigarette packet out of her pocket. Lit up a half-smoked joint. She inhaled, then offered it to Laura.

"Medicinal purposes."

Laura shook her head. "Nah."

"You sure?"

"Sure."

"Suit yourself."

Roz smoked the rest of the joint, rolling down the window to blow the smoke outside. When there was nothing left, she stubbed the joint out on the sole of her trainer. Put the butt in a plastic box in the glove compartment. The box was full of discarded cigarette butts that Laura had yet to put in the bin.

"This morning," Laura said, turning to her friend. "It really helped. Talking about what happened."

"Glad I could help, honey."

"If you ever want to talk, I'm happy to listen."

Roz stared through the windscreen, watching distant trees sway in the wind. "You already know what happened to me, sweetheart. Not all the details, but you've heard the story before. A hundred times or more."

"All the same," Laura said. "I'm here. If you want to talk–"

Roz pointed a finger at the driver's window. "We've got more pressing concerns."

"What?"

"Your man. He's leaving."

"Shit."

Laura spun around in the seat. Sure enough, Dirk's campervan was all closed up and ready to go. The engine purred and a puff of bluish-grey smoke shot out of the exhaust pipe. Dirk was behind the wheel, backing the van out of the narrow space. Once the Ducato was out, he turned it towards the road.

Laura fired up the California's engine, reversing out quickly. She hit the brakes when she heard a man yelling at her from the back of the van. High-pitched American accent.

"Are you crazy? Watch where you're going!"

Laura paid little attention to the insults. She steered the campervan towards the road, glancing in the mirror at the lanky man giving her the finger and still yelling. The brakes screeched as she reached the exit. Quick check for oncoming traffic. Laura pulled out, turning the wheel, racing after the Ducato that was already receding into the distance.

"There he is," Roz said. She pointed up ahead. "Heading north?"

Laura nodded. "Yep. This is day one of their holiday."

"How do you know that?"

"I've got my ways."

Roz smiled at that. "Day one, is it? One and done. If we have anything to do with it."

Laura gripped the wheel with both hands, eyes locked on the narrow, winding B-road. Most likely, the family were heading back to the A9 and would travel north from there. Maybe there'd be detours. Lots more stops.

I'll be right there with you, she thought.

Laura could feel Roz's eyes all over her. Two laser beams burning a hole in her skin.

"What is it?"

"Honey, before we do this…"

"What?"

"We need to talk about what we're doing here."

"Okay."

"And you need to be straight with me, okay?"

"Of course."

Roz ran a hand through her unwashed hair. She fidgeted with the end of her ponytail, then pointed again to the van in front of them. "You're one hundred percent sure about him. That's definitely Dirk in the campervan? It's not somebody else who looks like him?"

Laura shuddered at the thought. "You think I'm seeing things?"

"No, we just need to be sure."

"I'm sure. It's him alright. He's lost a bit of weight but I'd know that face and those black eyes anywhere."

Roz nodded, as if satisfied with Laura's response. "Good. Okay then, now that we've got that out of the way, it only leaves one question."

"What's the question?"

"How far are you willing to go?"

Laura turned the cold air back on inside the car. "What do you mean?"

"You know what I mean."

"I'm asking the question, Roz."

"Okay then," Roz said. "I'll try not to hurt your feelings. But you tried to kill him once today, right? You followed him up to the monument to end his life, but when it came to actually seeing it through, you couldn't do it."

Laura's grip on the wheel tightened. "Thanks for the reminder."

"Sorry hon, but this is no time for sugar-coating the truth. You *do* want to kill him, don't you? I mean, I didn't come out here just so you could punch him in the face or flush his head down the toilet. We're talking about giving him what he deserves. We're talking about cold-blooded murder, right?"

"Right. But–"

"But what?"

"Up on the hill," Laura said. "I realised that killing someone isn't easy. Even when you hate someone as much as I hate him. It's still taking a life and that's no small thing. Fuck, Roz. I just clammed up. I couldn't breathe. Couldn't move."

"You got scared."

"I know."

"It'll be fine," Roz said. Her aura of calm was unnerving, but it's what Laura needed. She was a basket case, her nerves shredded. She didn't need another person in the van flaking out beside her. She was serious about punishing Dirk.

"So, let me ask you again," Roz said. "How far are you willing to go?"

Laura felt like she was leaning over the edge of a tall cliff, a big drop waiting for her. "I'm willing to do whatever it takes."

She was surprised at how confident she sounded. A world away from what was going on inside.

Roz's voice was still calm. Her eyes still on the Ducato as she spoke. "Are you willing to break him?"

Laura's foot eased up on the accelerator. "Break him?"

"Killing him outright," Roz said. "That's too good for him. What's the point if he doesn't know what's hit him? I'm talking about something else. So that when we're done with him, he'll be begging us to put him out of his misery."

"You're talking about torturing him?"

Roz shrugged. "That's one way of putting it."

This was Laura's first glimpse at a side of Roz that she hadn't encountered before, but that she always knew existed. The ageing hippie chick, the free spirit who smoked weed and watched the sunset every night, she was gone. There was someone else sitting beside Laura now. The darkness that lived in Roz was front and centre. It was unsettling to experience, but Laura knew it's what she needed.

"Focus," Roz said. "Focus and motivation. That's what gets the job done today. And remember who we're talking about here. This guy turned off your old life like a switch. He lashed out. Took everything, hon. That's what he owes you. Plus interest."

"I know."

Roz pulled a cigarette out of the crumpled pack. She talked, the cigarette dancing between her lips. "What I'm saying sweetheart, is that revenge isn't pretty. This needs to get ugly before it becomes a beautiful thing. Very ugly. You won't feel good about it, not right away. But in time, who knows? You will sleep better though, I say that from experience. Knowing that you ended this bastard."

She lit up. Rolled down the window, blowing smoke outside.

"Think about it. What good would it do killing Dirk if his life was still shit, right? You'd be doing him a favour. It's charity. Much better this way. He's happy. Living the dream for all we know. Most importantly, you have something to take away."

"I can handle it," Laura said. Maybe it was the way Roz was talking about these things. Torture. Murder. Like it was a challenging hike and nothing more. Maybe it was just the natural progression of things after Laura's freak out on Fyrish Hill. But she felt better now. Calm. She saw the task clearly. Believed in her ability to carry it out.

"I know you can, hon. I wouldn't be here otherwise."

Roz smoked the cigarette down to the butt. After tossing the remains into Laura's plastic box, she rolled up the window, shutting out the cold air.

"How exactly are we going to do this?" Laura asked.

Roz looked at her friend. She rubbed both hands together for warmth. Or maybe it was excitement.

A smile crept onto her face.

"Don't you worry your pretty little head about it. I have a plan."

19

DIRK

The light was fading as Dirk drove through the gates of the Dornoch Caravan and Camping Park. Their accommodation for the night. No more than a two-minute drive from the local beach, the family's final stop after their first day on the road.

Prior to their arrival at the caravan park, Dirk, Diana and the kids had wandered around the Royal Burgh of Tain, stopping for lunch in the Royal Hotel, a historic-looking building at the head of High Street. Afterwards, they drove east to Portmahomack, a small village in the Tarbat Peninsula. Finally, they doubled back, continuing north up the A9 to Dornoch. As promised, the family visited the Witch's Stone, as well as the beach and a couple of other local sites listed in Diana's guide book. The kids remained in good spirits, despite all the walking. Both Dirk and Diana were happy with how it went.

After checking in with Tracey and Matt, the friendly

staff members at reception, Dirk parked the Ducato at the rear of the caravan park.

The kids didn't waste any time when it came to exploring their surroundings. There were plenty of facilities in the caravan park for visitors: a shop, launderette, free showers, games room and more.

Isla dragged the side door open, telling her parents she was going for a walk. Joe was right behind her, mumbling something about snooker tables and the games room. They went in opposite directions.

Dirk and Diana were only too happy to let the kids go wandering. The park was safe enough and they needed a break too. After freshening up, they unfolded a couple of deckchairs outside and opened a bottle of wine. They sat under a glorious sky that looked like something out of a painting. The clouds scattered above the caravan park were hazy cotton balls, lounging on a violet backdrop. Hints of gold crept in at the edges.

They clinked glasses.

"To us," Dirk said.

Diana raised her glass. "And to day one. Done and dusted."

She sipped the Pinot Noir, then fell back into the deckchair with a sigh. Her joints cracked, loud enough to make them both laugh.

"Oh God. Do you still love me?"

Dirk put a hand on her leg. "Even though you're old and crackly?"

She nodded. "Even though I'm old and crackly."

Dirk brought the rim of the glass to his nostrils. He inhaled the fruity aroma, pretending like he knew what he was doing. "More than ever."

"You mean that mister?"

"Of course."

Dirk's eyes combed the surroundings. The other people occupying the caravan park looked harmless enough. Why wouldn't they? Mild-mannered tourists. Families. Retirees who'd chosen to spend their later years on the road, seeing new things, going places. Everyone was in good form tonight. Some of them waved at Dirk and Diana. There were a couple of casual introductions, but nothing intrusive. There was a mood of relaxation in the air that was palpable.

Diana tilted her head back. So relaxed she was deflating. "No midges tonight either. That's a win."

"Hmmm."

She gave Dirk a knowing smile.

"The kids are fine. Stop worrying."

"I know."

"Something else bothering you?"

"No."

"Seems like you're on edge."

"No, I'm fine."

There *was* something. But Dirk couldn't pin it down. A restlessness. Probably nothing. He took a sip. It was a delicious wine from Chile, a special (and expensive) purchase that he'd been hoping to save for later in the trip, perhaps a final night on the road toast for all the family. Even the kids. But Diana had insisted on opening the bottle now. And if her track record was anything to go by, the bottle would be empty before nine o'clock. Maybe that's what was bothering him. Dirk didn't like it when his wife drank too much. She got flirty. Touchy-feely. It drove him crazy sometimes.

"You're not thinking about Court and the kids, are you?" Diana asked.

Dirk frowned. "Where did that come from?" His voice

was high-pitched. Almost squeaky. He sounded like someone who'd been caught red-handed.

Diana shrugged. "I don't know. You must think about them."

"My family's right here," Dirk said, taking her hand and squeezing gently. "With you, Isla and Joe. This is everything I ever wanted."

"We make you happy?"

He nodded. "I've never been happier."

"Glad to hear it."

Diana emptied her glass. Put it down beside the chair. She leaned over towards Dirk, tracing the tip of her finger along his thigh. The caress showed no sign of stopping as it travelled further north.

"Woah," Dirk said, laughing nervously. He looked around to see if anyone was watching. "What are you doing?"

"Are you complaining, Dirk?"

"No, but–"

Dirk blushed. He was convinced that everyone in the caravan park was watching. That's what he'd be doing if a middle-aged couple started acting like a pair of lust-filled teenagers after half a glass of wine.

God, that was his father's voice. His old man was trapped in his head.

He checked. No one was watching.

"I'm a little tipsy," Diana said. "That didn't take long."

She stood up, grabbing the wine glass off the ground. Leaning over, she kissed Dirk on the lips. On the neck. Pressing down hard. He could smell the perfume on her skin.

She whispered in his ear.

"The kids won't be back for a while."

"We don't know that."

"Makes it all the more dangerous then, doesn't it?"

Before Dirk could say anything, Diana was pulling him off the chair. Dirk stood up. Saw the bulge at his crotch. By now, he was past caring if anyone was watching. At Diana's request, he picked up the wine bottle. With their hands locked together, they walked towards the campervan.

20

LAURA

It was a little after two o'clock in the morning when Roz and Laura put the masks over their head. The rest of the caravan park was silent.

"This fucking thing stinks," Laura said, her voice muffled. She'd cut a vertical gash in the sack-mask where her mouth should be, but it still sounded like she was buried underground when she talked. "Smells like rotten fruit in here."

"They're your sacks," Roz said. "What were you keeping in them?"

"Nothing. They've been lying around in the van forever. I honestly don't know why I took them from Masons."

Roz adjusted the sack over her head, pulling at the sides. She secured the two large slits at the top over her eyes. They slipped down a little, sending her into the dark. "Bloody hell. This thing's all over the place."

"It's the best I could do on short notice."

"Laura, we don't need masks. Not with *this* plan."

"We discussed this. I want masks. At least, at the beginning. I don't do this sort of thing every day, you know?"

"Okay, okay. Are you ready?"

"I'm ready."

"Sure about that?"

"Stop asking me that, Roz. I'm not going to choke again."

It was Laura's turn to fidget with her mask. The disguise wasn't comfortable and the coarse burlap reeked to the point of distraction. It itched too. But Laura needed it. Putting the mask on was like flipping a switch. It was the permission she needed to become someone else. This was how she'd make it through the night. Roz's plan was brutal. They hadn't even started and Laura was already doubting her ability to see it through.

It had been a long day. They'd followed Dirk's family to Tain, Portmahomack, then finally here to Dornoch. Watched as the happy family strolled along the beach, seemingly without a care in the world. Eating chips. Drinking Coca-Cola, taking in all the pretty colours that flowered on the horizon.

It hurt Laura to see Dirk so contented. It *physically* hurt.

Finally, the family left the beach and checked into Dornoch caravan park.

Despite the fact it was summer, Laura and Roz had no problems getting into the busy caravan park. They were both well-acquainted with the owners, particularly Tracey. The unspoken rule, according to Tracey, was that if either Laura or Roz turned up unannounced, there'd always be somewhere to park, even if it wasn't a proper pitch.

They'd spent most of the evening watching the Ducato. Watching, watching, watching. It had been ninety percent of the day. Just two friends, strolling around the campsite, minding their own business. Following the same route, but never getting too close to their campervan. The two kids were gone. Dirk and his wife sat outside, enjoying their picturesque surroundings. Nice bottle of wine. At one point, they went inside holding hands, closing the door behind them. The Ducato trembled. It was obvious what they were up to.

Bastard, Laura thought.

She hadn't had sex in years. Worst of all, she'd lost all desire for it. There was nothing. No feeling.

Laura's anger bubbled up all throughout the evening surveillance. She wanted a drink. There was a six-pack of beer in the campervan fridge. Maybe it was a three-pack now. There was also a bottle of whisky in the cupboard. Half-gone, but enough to get Laura shitfaced if she mixed it with the beer.

But it wasn't going to happen. She had to keep a clear head. There was a long night ahead of them.

A *hard* night.

It felt like days since she'd slept. Or eaten something.

They'd watched the Ducato until darkness swept over the caravan park. Until all the family were back inside. At a little after ten o'clock, the lights went out. Laura and Roz returned to the California to wait it out. They wouldn't come back out until the park was silent, until all the lights were switched off.

"There's no turning back," Roz said to Laura. With the mask on, the giant woman looked terrifying. Knowing what she intended for the family, she *was* terrifying. "When it gets tough, remember what he did. To you, to your family."

Laura nodded.

"I'll remember."

At 2.07am, they walked across the eerie campsite. Rifles in hand. Silent as ghosts, their feet not making a sound on the grass. Whatever fear had crippled Laura at Fyrish Monument, it was gone. She was ready. *Motivation*, she told herself on the walk over. *Remember your motivation.* That was her mantra.

Roz's presence was a godsend. Laura could do this, but she couldn't do it alone.

They stopped outside the Ducato. Roz glanced around, conducting a final check of the park. She leaned forward, whispering in Laura's ear. Her voice so quiet that Laura could barely hear it.

"You want justice?"

Laura nodded.

"Then forget the law," Roz said. There was bite in her voice. "We can do whatever we want. We *are* the law. We *are* justice."

Laura adjusted the sack. Made sure the eyeholes and mouth were in the right place.

She nodded at Roz.

"I'm ready."

21

LAURA

Laura knocked on the door.

It sounded like a battering ram hitting the Ducato. Quick look over the shoulder. Surely, she'd just woken up everyone else in the caravan park.

Nothing. No lights. No sound.

They were good.

"What's taking them so long?" Roz asked. Her voice was a distorted hiss through the mouth hole. She stepped closer to the van. Was about to rap her sledgehammer knuckles on the door when Laura grabbed her arm. It felt like grabbing an oak tree.

"Let me handle this."

Roz took a step back. "Go for it."

Laura positioned her head closer to the door. Were those voices she could hear inside the Ducato? Were they awake? Aware that someone was outside? She could feel the frantic galloping of her heart.

She knocked again. Softer this time.

"Excuse me. Is anyone awake? It's Tracey from reception. Sorry to bother you at such a late hour."

Roz was laughing behind her mask. She whispered. "Ehh, Tracey's from Liverpool. Do the accent!"

"Oh shit."

Laura gave a thumbs up. She knocked again. This time, she remembered to include the Liverpudlian accent.

"Excuse me. Reception."

The two women flinched at a sudden thudding noise inside the van.

Laura thought it sounded big. Most likely, it was only heavy feet hitting off the floor. Maybe jumping off a bunk or something. Half-asleep, their mind still circling the airport. Laura and Roz took a step back from the van. A light flickered on inside the Ducato. Laura felt a sudden jolt of terror. Was she about to experience some form of paralysis again at the crucial moment?

Footsteps approached.

The sound of hushed voices. Labouring not to be heard.

Laura fought back the sudden urge to run away. That's what her mind was screaming at her to do. This wasn't just a dark fantasy anymore. This was real. It was happening. This was the resurrection of her failure at the monument. There was no way she could go through with Roz's vengeful plan. It was too much, even for Dirk. She looked at Roz. Searching for that shine of reassuring confidence in Roz's eyes. The same confidence that was slipping away from Laura like sand through an egg timer.

It was there.

"We can do this," Roz whispered. She must have seen the doubt in Laura, even through the mask. "You'll be fine."

Laura nodded. She inhaled and exhaled slowly, no

longer concerned about the smell of rotten fruit inside the sack.

They heard a man's voice inside the Ducato. He sounded groggy, but close. Dirk. Was he still half asleep? Or was he fully alert, aware that something was wrong with the receptionist knocking on their door at this time? Maybe Dirk knew it wasn't the receptionist. Laura squeezed down on the rifle butt. Kept the barrel on the door. She glanced right. Noticed there was a roller blind on the window beside the door. *Shit*, she thought. All Dirk had to do was raise the blind a few inches and he'd see two masked figures with guns at the door.

Laura had to put him at ease. Make sure he didn't check.

"Who is it?" Dirk asked.

He *was* right behind the door. Which meant he could lift that roller blind at any moment.

Laura felt a cold shudder. Her eyes darted back and forth between the door and window.

"Hello again sir," she said. "This is Tracey from the overnight reception. We met earlier this evening when I checked you in. I'm so sorry to wake you at such a late hour but there's been an urgent issue with the electricity supply around the caravan park and we just wanted to check that everything was working okay at this pitch."

There was a long pause. Laura could almost hear the bastard's brain ticking in there, trying to figure this thing out.

"It's working fine," Dirk said. "The light's on."

"Everything's okay, is it?"

"Yes."

Laura's sweaty palm slipped down the rifle butt. The mask wasn't in place either. Eyeholes kept moving off her eyes.

Hotel room. Don't Drink Girl. Tommy. Career in tatters. Life ruined.

"Do you need anything else?" Dirk asked. "Or is that it?"

Roz gave Laura a nudge on the arm.

"That's great you've got power," Laura said. "Yeah, maybe you could also check the–"

She covered the mouth hole with her hand, muffling her voice. Kept talking. Then she let go at the end.

"...for me please?"

A pause.

"Check the what?" Dirk asked. "I didn't catch that."

Laura repeated the trick. There was a loud groan from inside the van.

"This is it," Roz whispered. She stretched to her full godlike height, bracing herself for action. "Get ready, hon."

The sound of a key turning in the lock. As loud as the battering ram that was Laura's knuckles on the door.

Laura clamped her feet to the grass. Kept the gun on the door. All the fears and doubts of Fyrish were gone. Swallowed in a black hole.

No more running.

It was on.

22

DIRK

"Dad, there's someone at the door."

Isla's voice called to Dirk, pulling him out of deep sleep. At first, he couldn't move. His body was a block of human-shaped lead. He was lying in his bunk, looking up at the blank void above his head, waiting for it to take the shape of something. All the activities of day one, combined with half a bottle of wine and an unexpected sexual encounter with Diana, had worn Dirk out.

"Dad? Did you hear what I said?"

"Hmmm."

"Someone's at the door."

Dirk heard the urgency in his stepdaughter's voice. That did it. A sudden jolt of fear worked better than any alarm clock and he sat up in bed, surrounded by darkness. He felt the cold air inside the van. Pinching at the skin on his arms.

"W-w-what?"

The others began to stir in their beds. Joe was moaning in the bunk above Isla. Diana was directly above Dirk, the mattress creaking as she tried to shake loose from the grip of sleep. Dirk flinched when his wife's floppy arm appeared at the side. He looked to the right, his eyes slowly adjusting to the dark. Another cold shiver down his spine.

Isla was sitting on the edge of the bunk. The whites of her eyes, staring towards the kitchen. Towards the door.

"There's someone out there."

Dirk rubbed his eyes. He was aware of a dull, gnawing headache at the temples. As he was about to throw the covers back, Dirk realised he was sporting a massive erection. He hesitated, even though it was pitch black.

Wow, he thought. *So much energy tonight.*

"What is it, Dirk?" Diana asked in a groggy voice.

"It's fine," he said, staring into the kitchen. "It's probably the wind. Or rain hitting the window."

He waited. Maybe it was an animal. There were bound to be foxes running around in this neck of the woods, making all sorts of noises. There were always strange sounds in new places, especially at night when everything was quiet. Isla was so easily spooked.

"Dad?"

"It's alright, Isla."

"I heard something."

"Okay. I'll have a look."

It was only right. He was the man of the house after all. It was Dirk's duty to make sure that everyone else felt safe. He swung his legs over the side of the bed. They landed hard, like he'd misjudged the distance. Damn, it was cold. He stood up, his back facing the others. Thank God, the erection was on its way down. Thanks to the cold.

He took a step forward, fingers grasping for the light switch. Before he could find it, he heard a noise. A woman's voice. It was coming from outside.

"Excuse me."

Isla wasn't hearing things. There *was* someone out there. What the hell was this? Who'd be standing at a stranger's door in the middle of the night, calling into their campervan van like that?

Had to be trouble.

His brain was a soup of sluggish outrage.

"What the–?"

"Who is it?" Diana asked.

Dirk heard the tremor in his wife's voice. He looked at the kids. Joe was still wriggling around in slow motion, trying to wake up. Isla was perched on the edge of her bed. Eyes locked on Dirk's every move.

"I'll deal with it," he said, addressing the others. "Don't worry, it's nothing."

If only he could sound convincing.

He spun around, searching for his phone on the table. Then he realised that his bedside table, where he usually left his phone charging overnight, was back in his bedroom in Edinburgh. *Damn it*, Dirk thought. *Where did I leave it?* Where were the light switches in this bloody campervan? Everything was unfamiliar, especially so after waking up in the dark. Robbed of sleep. At this rate, he'd need a torch just to find the light switch.

Then it came to him. He'd tucked his phone under the pillow before falling asleep. He lifted the pillow up. Grabbed the phone, looked at the time.

"Ten past two in the morning."

Diana gasped. "What the hell?"

Dirk stared into the darkness of the kitchen.

"Something must be wrong," Diana said, speaking in a hushed voice. "What if somebody needs help?"

Dirk rubbed his eyes. "I'll deal with it."

He listened to the woman's voice at the door. She was still whispering which meant that if it was an emergency, it was a quiet one.

"That's the woman from reception," Isla said, a sudden tone of relief spilling into her voice. "The English one."

"There you go. Nothing to worry about."

Dirk walked through the kitchen, finding the light switch on the wall. He squinted at the light. Felt like he'd walked straight into the sun. He kept walking, trying to shake off the cobwebs in his mind. As he approached the door, Dirk glanced at the knife rack beside the toaster.

Don't be silly, he thought.

Still, he'd confirm it one more time. Just to be sure.

"Who is it?" Dirk asked, leaning his shoulder against the door. He glanced at the roller blind to his right. He could pull the cord. Peek outside. Looking down, he saw there was still a bulge in his boxer shorts. Not all the way down, not yet. What if the woman was carrying a torch? He'd never live it down.

"Hi, this is Tracey from the overnight reception. Sorry to bother you at such a late hour but there's been an issue with the electricity supply and we just wanted to check everything was working okay."

Dirk glanced at the ceiling bulb. Then, a quick scan around the kitchen. There was a microwave with a digital clock and the numbers were still on display, reminding him of the atrocious hour.

"It's working fine. The light's on."

He motioned his head closer to the door. "Do you need anything else? Or is that it?"

There was a short pause.

"That's great you've got power. Yeah, maybe you could also check the...for me please?"

Dirk's face folded into a frown. "Check the what? I didn't catch that."

More mumbling behind the door.

Dirk rubbed his eyes, looking down at his crotch. The bulge was gone. All clear. Okay. Best get this sorted. He turned the key in the lock, stepped back and pulled the door open.

There wasn't enough time to scream.

23

LAURA

"Get back!" Laura said, charging inside the van. She didn't recognise her own voice. "Hands up in the air."

Dirk's eyes bulged in terror. His hands shot above his head as he backed off to the other side of the van. His mouth shuddered as if he was trying to speak. A faint whimper was all he could manage.

Roz was right behind Laura, hurrying up the single step and barging through the doorway. It sounded like an elephant stampede. She closed the campervan door behind her. Turned the key in the lock.

Both women pointed their Remingtons at Dirk. A dark stain appeared at the front of his shorts. The drip of urine hitting the floor.

"Nice," Roz said.

Dirk didn't even seem to notice the mess. His arms were still up. Fingertips scraping off the ceiling. "P-p-please. What do you w-want?"

Laura stood with her back against the door. There was

just enough light in the kitchen to make out what was going
on. The others were in the bedroom. She counted three
heads. They had their hands up. Dirk's wife and the boy
were on the two top bunks. Legs hanging over the side. The
girl was on the lower bunk, underneath the boy. Her naked
feet were on the floor. She clutched a pillow to her chest.
Stared at the intruders. Eyes wide with fear.

"W-what do you want?" Dirk asked for a second time. He
was standing in a puddle of hot piss.

"Shut up," Roz said. Her voice was a distorted growl
under the mask. She came forward, jamming the muzzle
against the side of Dirk's head. This elicited a shriek from
the bedroom. "Try anything. You and your family are dead.
Got it?"

Dirk nodded.

Laura was sweating under the mask. Damn eyeslits kept
sliding off-centre. Putting her in the dark unless she kept
fixing it. The mask had been a rush job and because of the
nerves, not a particularly good one. She'd barely been able
to concentrate. Roz was right. They didn't need masks but
Laura still wanted them.

"Everyone take it nice and easy," she said, after pulling
the mask into position. "Nice and easy, okay?"

Laura doublechecked the campervan door. Made sure it
was locked just in case someone tried to run.

"Do what we say. Nobody gets hurt."

"What do you want?" the woman said, her voice trembling. "What do you want from us? We'll give you whatever
you want, okay?"

It was Roz who answered. "You'll find out soon enough."

"Do you want money?" the woman asked. "The van? You
can have it. Whatever it is you want, you can have it. We'll
cooperate."

"Shut up," Roz said, turning her rifle on the people in the back. Laura looked at her. Hard to believe that Roz could point a gun at children like that. Her finger hovering over the trigger. Even in a situation as fucked up as this one.

The boy made a high-pitched whimpering noise. He sounded like a frightened animal.

Roz looked at Laura. Gave her a nod as if to say, *continue*.

Laura walked over to Dirk, making sure to avoid the wet patch at his feet. She pressed the barrel into his chest. Pushed hard. The impact sent Dirk back several paces, but he remained on his feet. She hit him again.

"Stop!" the woman yelled from the back.

Dirk doubled over, made a loud wheezing noise as if all the air had been knocked out of him. He staggered backwards through the kitchen. Legs like jelly. Off-balance, working his way to the back of the van.

"P-p-please."

Dirk stood in the doorway, shielding his family from the intruders. It looked like a stiff breeze would blow him over.

"Please don't–"

Laura chased after him. She pointed the Remington at his head. Every time she looked at his face, she was back in the hotel room in Glasgow. Inhaling his smoke. Watching him drink from a silver hip flask. Dead-eyed. She was naked and helpless, cowering under the sheets. She was the Don't Drink Girl.

"Bastard."

Laura spun the rifle around. She lashed out, striking the butt off the side of Dirk's head. She put real force behind it. The power coming up from her legs. There was a loud cracking noise. Dirk's shoulders dropped. He went down like a demolished skyscraper, hitting his shoulder off the kitchen countertop.

The woman and two kids shrieked but Roz pointed the rifle at them. She pressed a finger to her lips, urging them to be quiet.

"Shhh."

Dirk landed on his back. Sprawled out, arms and legs everywhere. He was still conscious, groaning in pain.

Laura adjusted the mask yet again. She looked down at the ragged shape of the man. Damp crotch. Bloody head. She could do this. *Be like Roz*, she urged herself. Something had changed in Roz. Dormant anger was bubbling its way to the surface. That was strength. That's what Laura needed tonight to see Roz's plan through to the end. It wasn't going to be pretty. It was going to haunt Laura for the rest of her life. But there was no going back. Dirk had to pay. He had to suffer. And the others? The woman, the two kids? Wrong place, wrong time. Wrong husband, wrong father. Tommy had suffered. Laura's mum and dad suffered, all because of him. Her friends too.

Everyone gets hurt.

That's how it works.

The woman clamped a hand over her mouth, desperate to scream. Eyes ballooning in terror. Roz took a step towards her and the children. Daring her to try something. The woman reached out for the semi-conscious Dirk on the floor. At the same time, she was inching her body to the left, trying to block Roz's view of the children.

Tears streamed down her cheeks.

"What do you want from us?"

"I want you to come with me," Laura said. "You and your children."

The woman shook her head. She was about to speak but Laura cut her off.

"You don't understand. I'm not asking."

Laura looked at the kids. The girl was still hugging the pillow. Not looking at anything or anyone in particular. Up on the top, the boy's eyes were shut. Looked like he was swaying back and forth.

"Please don't separate us," the woman said.

Dirk was groaning on the floor. Sounded like he was trying to speak, but a barrage of stuttered grunts was all he could manage.

"You'll be okay," Laura said to the woman. *A lie.* "We're going outside, you and me, along with the kids. We'll walk in single file with me. And you'll be quiet. Won't you?"

The woman nodded. "Yes."

Dirk was still trying to make words. "*Ugghhh. Dooont. Naaaaoo.*"

Roz leaned over the man. The muzzle of her Remington inching towards his mouth. "You'd better shut up."

The woman wiped tears from her eyes. She coughed. Stared at Laura, clasping her hands as if in prayer.

"Just tell me. What do you want?"

Laura looked at the woman. "I just told you. Let's go. Everyone on their feet. And remember – if you scream, I'll shoot your children."

The woman's body slumped in defeat. But she sprang into action. Helped the kids off their bunks one at a time. At Laura's command, they put some clothes and shoes on. The boy started crying again. His sister, her arm wrapped around his shoulder, pulled him close. At their mother's signal, they walked towards the doorway where Laura was waiting.

"We're going for a little walk," the woman said. "Just a little walk."

Laura pointed a finger at the boy.

"I need him to be quiet."

The woman looked at Laura like she was the devil. Then, she leaned over the boy. Spoke softly into his ear.

"Joe, sweetheart. Listen to me. Can you be quiet for me? That's a good boy. There's nothing to worry about, I swear. No need to cry. She's not going to hurt us, you heard her, didn't you? We're just going for a little walk across the caravan park. Look at me honey. Look at *me*."

Joe made a loud sniffing noise. He nodded.

"I'll keep an eye on this one," Roz said, standing over Dirk.

Laura nodded. "We need to restrain him."

She shoved a hand into her coat pocket. Pulled out the set of steel handcuffs she'd brought from the junk-yard that was the back of the Grand California. She'd used these handcuffs six years ago to surprise Tommy on his thirtieth birthday, fulfilling one of her fiancée's longstanding sexual fantasies – that of being hand-cuffed to the bed. Laura wasn't sure why she'd brought them to the Highlands. They were a painful reminder of her past life. A reminder of the happiest she'd ever been.

She knelt down in front of Dirk. Grabbed an arm, helping him up to his feet.

"C'mon, Dirk. Let's get up, shall we?"

"How do you know his name?" the woman asked, standing at the door.

"Quiet," Roz snapped.

Dirk howled in protest as Laura pulled on his arm. He got up, still wobbly on his feet. Laura steered him over to the nearest bunk bed while Roz kept her rifle on the woman and kids at the door. They watched the situation unfold in horrified silence.

Laura pushed Dirk back down onto the floor. She took

his wrist. Stretched it out. Cuffed him to the foot of the bunk bed nearest the kitchen.

"If you try anything while I'm gone," Laura whispered, "I'll kill your family. So don't be a silly billy. Be a good boy for my friend. Okay?"

His eyes were swirling. But he nodded.

Laura gave him a pat on the head. "Good."

"He won't try anything," Roz said in a gruff voice. She was a giant silhouette framed in the kitchen doorway. "I'll make sure of that."

Laura walked back into the light. She looked at the woman. "Ready?"

"Ready," the woman said, glancing past Laura towards her husband. Dirk was a battered wreck on the floor. His head rolled around in a slow, clockwise motion. Looked like it was trying to unscrew itself from the shoulders.

Laura gestured for the others to walk ahead of her. "Go. Unlock the door and step outside. Slowly. Then, walk straight ahead. Light, easy pace. Remember what happens if you try to run, make a sound or pull any stunts."

She tapped the Remington barrel.

"No bluffing."

The woman, her arms wrapped around the two children's shoulders, turned to the door. Their heads were lowered. Eyes to the ground. Looked like they were walking to the gallows for a family execution.

Laura turned back to Roz, who was leaning up against the nearest bunk bed, lighting up a cigarette.

"I won't be long."

"Don't worry about us," Roz said. "We'll be fine."

Dirk's back was pressed up against the side of the bed. Head still rolling from side to side.

"P-p-please...don't..."

Laura turned her back on the man. She walked outside into the fresh air and breathed it in. She followed the woman and children as they began their trek across the caravan park. Dirk's voice was the last thing she heard before closing the door.

"Please...please d-d-don't hurt my family."

24

LAURA

Laura walked behind the woman and her children. Every step, slow and careful. Like she was surrounded by landmines.

The rest of the caravan park was silent; it was the sort of silence that suggested they were hundreds of miles from civilisation. The four people walked under a sky that was black, speckled with stars. The soft crunch of their feet off the grass was the only sound. Laura's Remington was on their backs. Heart racing. She envisioned the worst. What if one of the kids freaked out and started screaming? What if the woman thought that alerting the entire caravan park was their only chance of survival?

Would she shoot them?

Could she?

What did it matter? If Roz's plan came to fruition, they'd be dead before sunrise.

Her eyes darted back and forth between all the caravans and campervans that surrounded them. So many. Dark silhouettes, tall and silent. Laura hoped that everyone inside was asleep. All it took for things to start going wrong was that one insomniac lying awake, listening as Laura and her captives trudged past. They get up. Peer out from behind the curtains. There wasn't much light, but there was enough to see a masked figure marching three people across the site at gunpoint.

Fortunately for Laura, they made it back to the Grand California without incident. Laura whispered instructions, telling them to line up and put their backs against the van. Then, she opened the door. The smell of whisky and tobacco hit her like a slap on the face.

Laura switched on the light. Ushered the family inside. Once they were in, she pointed them towards the bedroom at the back.

"Sit down," Laura said, pointing to the unmade bed.

She closed the door while the others walked in silence to the bedroom. Locked it. Checked the handle three times. Then, she adjusted the mask, pulling at one side to slot the eyeholes back in place.

Pause.

Deep breath.

She was doing okay.

Laura switched on the bedroom light. The three captives were sitting on the bed as ordered. The kids positioned on either side of their mother, all three of them looking tired and frightened.

"Please don't do this," the woman said. "We've done you no harm."

Laura knelt down at the doorway. Began unzipping the large duffel bag on the floor. "Right now, I need you to be quiet."

"Please–"

"Quiet."

She pulled out a long coil of rope from inside the bag.

"Tie them together," Laura said to the woman. She pointed at the kids. "Okay guys, I want you to sit with your backs touching. Mum's going to get up and she's going to wrap the rope around you and she's going to do it right. I'll be watching to make sure she does it right. Backs touching. That clear?"

The woman shook her head. Her eyes pleaded with Laura.

"I can't do this."

Laura took a step closer, raising the rifle. "I said, is that clear?"

"Yes."

Laura nodded. "Good. What's your name?"

"Diana."

"Okay. Get to work Diana."

Laura tossed the rope at Diana's feet. She didn't know if Dirk's wife was any good at tying knots but it was time to find out. As long as the knot was strong enough to hold the two children together and prevent them from slipping loose, it would do. The last thing Laura needed was one of the little bastards, or both of them, wriggling loose while she was away. To create a disturbance. To raise the alarm.

Diana picked up the rope. There was a vacant look on her face as she went to work, methodically looping the thin rope around the children's torsos. Talking quietly to them, telling them over and over that it'd be alright.

Laura pulled at the shitty mask. Found the eyeholes. She watched closely, making sure that Diana wasn't purposefully leaving the rope loose enough to slip off.

"Tighter."

Diana glared at Laura. Now her eyes burned. "I don't

want to hurt them for God's sake. I can restrain them without hurting them, can't I?"

"They'll live. What's the girl's name?"

"Isla."

Laura nodded. "Isla, there's no need to look so scared. You can put your back against the wall once the rope's tied. You'll be more comfortable that way."

Did the girl recognise Laura's voice from Skiach? There was nothing that gave Laura the impression that Isla knew her. The poor girl was sickly-white around the face. Stiff as a board. Legs trembling.

"You'll be okay," Laura said. Again, not convincing.

There was a noise outside that made Laura flinch. Sounded like the flapping of wings over the campervan. Maybe an owl. She hoped that's all it was.

"Why?" Diana asked. She narrowed her eyes, straining, as if trying to see Laura's face behind the mask. "Are you ever going to explain? What did we do to deserve *this*?"

"What's the boy's name?" Laura asked.

Diana's shoulders slumped in defeat.

"Joe."

"Joe," Laura said. "Quit puffing out your chest like that. You wouldn't be doing that to make the rope looser, would you? Did your mum tell you to do that?"

The muscles on Diana's neck tightened.

"Back to work," Laura said.

Diana continued tying up the children.

Laura watched from the doorway. "That's it. That's good. Make sure you leave the ends free for the knot."

"I know how to tie a rope," Diana snapped.

"Yeah, I suppose you do."

Diana tied off a perfect square knot. It was better than anything Laura could have done. The kids weren't going anywhere. Now that they were tied up, Laura wondered how Roz was getting on in the Ducato with Dirk.

Damn it, she thought.

Fucking mask. Still slipping down her face.

A dog barked from afar. Laura flinched. Instinct forced her head to turn to the window. It was a split-second reaction.

"BITCH!"

Diana was up off the bed. Running straight at her. There was no time to bring the Remington into play before Diana was clawing at Laura's mask, securing a grip, pulling it downwards. The eyeholes were gone. Laura was plunged into darkness. She had no idea if Diana was acting out of unfiltered motherly instinct, the lioness protecting her cubs, or if she'd noticed the mask slipping down Laura's face several times already. Had she been planning a surprise attack all this time?

"Crazy fucking bitch!" Diana yelled, throwing a barrage of punches.

Laura could feel the blows landing on her face and arms. They weren't hard but the shots were relentless. Endless slaps. Arm punches. Then it stopped. Laura, still in the dark, was jerked forward as Diana tried to grab the rifle out of her hands. Laura felt a surge of panic. She doubled down, gripping the barrel tight. Her fingers were sweaty and slippery. It felt like she was being pulled in all directions.

She couldn't lose the gun.

"Mum!" Isla screamed.

Too much noise, Laura thought. *Someone will come.*

The violent tug-of-war continued at the back of the Grand California. Laura's palms and fingers were too damp. Diana was strong. Stronger than Laura. She could feel the weapon slipping out of her grasp.

"No!"

Her voice was lost in the sack.

Diana was still coming forward, throwing wild kicks. Hitting Laura on the shins.

"Let go you bitch."

Laura was still in the dark, but she could hear Diana breathing heavily. The assault had tapered off slightly. But Diana wasn't about to let exhaustion get in the way of saving her family. That much was clear.

The two women had a hold of each other. They staggered forward, then back across the bedroom at speed, losing balance and yet somehow staying on their feet. Laura's back slammed against the wall on several occasions. She felt a jolt. The lights going on and off again. The pain would come later.

The wrestling match continued until eventually, they toppled to the floor. The landing was another jolt to Laura's senses. That one would really hurt.

"Mum!" Joe yelled.

Laura couldn't see. She couldn't breathe. There was only the foul-smelling sack pressed tight against her face. She felt the full weight of Diana slamming on top of her and once again, trying to wrestle the Remington free from her grip.

"Let go! It's over."

Laura felt helpless. Was Diana right? Was it over? She was on the floor, on the wrong end of a ferocious scramble with a desperate mother. *Give it up*, said the voice in her head. *Give it up. You gambled. You lost.*

Then it happened.

A surge of reserve energy. The lactic acid build-up halted, at least for now. It came out of nowhere, an explosion of rage that brought Laura back with a fighting chance. Just as the butt of the Remington was slipping through her fingers. Laura knew what would happen if she lost the gun. Police. Arrest. Jail. No one would ever know or care what Dirk had done to her. She would be the monster. The bad guy. Forever.

Dirk would win.

The bastard would win. And he'd live happy.

Laura loosened her grip on both the barrel and butt. This time, instead of pulling the rifle towards her, she let go. Another roll of the dice. One that could've gone badly wrong. Diana gasped, the momentum taking her by surprise. All Laura could hear in the darkness of the mask was a loud thud that rocked the Grand California. Diana's weight was off her. Laura sat up, light and free. She pulled the mask over her head. Diana was on the other side of the room, doubled over in pain. One hand pressed against the back of her neck, as if she'd smashed it off the bedroom wall. Eyes closed. Groaning. Trying to get back to her feet, battling through a wall of pain.

The rifle was on the floor. In between the two women.

Laura jumped to her feet. It was a fifty-fifty grab from here. Quickest feet wins.

"No," Diana said, sobbing. Her voice cracked with desperation. She reached a hand for the Remington and winced. She was unable to cover the distance. The realisation that she'd lost was all over her face. "Please."

Laura scooped up the Remington, taking control of the room. At the same time, she lowered the mask, even though they'd seen her face. A face that, right now, felt like it was on fire. It was pointless having the damn mask on. And yet, Laura wasn't ready to let it go.

She jammed the muzzle against Diana's forehead. Diana winced, then closed her eyes, as if preparing for the worst.

The kids were crying on the bed.

"That was stupid," Laura said, trying to get her breath back. She felt the sweat dripping down her back. Now she was starting to feel those punches around the ribs. The kicks to the shins. Superficial wounds, but annoying.

The crying behind her was getting louder. Surely, somebody in of the neighbouring campervans or caravans would hear the noise. There'd be footsteps. Concerned voices. A knock on the door.

"Shut the fuck up!" Laura hissed. "Shut the fuck up or I'll blow your mum's brains all over the wall."

Did I really just say that?

Isla and Joe's eyes bulged with terror. But they fell silent.

I'm the monster, Laura thought. *It's my turn now. I'm the monster.*

Diana sat up on the floor with a groan. A hand still pressing down on her neck. Tears streamed down a face that had aged ten years since the family's arrival at the caravan park. Her shoulders were stooped. Eyes heavy with defeat.

"What do you want?"

"I want you to keep your voice down."

Diana nodded. She was still out of breath, her chest heaving up and down. She put her hands up, as if surrendering once and for all. "Okay. I'm sorry. But please, tell me why you're doing this to us. I have to know. Is it just random? Did we do something?"

The smell of the mask made Laura want to throw up. She took a step closer to Diana. Leaned over the woman.

"What do you know about the man you married?"

Diana wiped the tears off her face. "What?"

"What do you *really* know about Dirk? About his past. About who he is. The things he's done."

"I know I love him."

"Is he a good man?"

There was a look of bewilderment on Diana's face. "What are you talking about? Has...has this got something to do with Dirk?"

There was a long silence.

"You deserve an explanation," Laura said. "You all do. But this isn't the right time."

"Please talk to me. If he's done something–"

"Stand up," Laura said. "Stand up and turn around. Hands behind your back."

Diana sighed, but did as she was told. Her movement was slow. Exhausted. All the fight seemed to have left her. "Please, what did he do? Tell me about Dirk."

Laura didn't answer. She backed off towards the doorway, then pulled out a second, shorter coil of rope from the bag. This was her chance to secure these people, now that Diana was beaten mentally and physically. Lowering the gun on the floor, Laura hurried over and began to tie Diana's wrists together. Then she did the ankles.

"You sit down on the floor."

That was it. Done. The kids were tied up on the bed and Diana slumped on the floor beside them. The only thing left was to gag them. Laura took a step back, surveying her handiwork. Then she turned away. The look in their eyes, she couldn't bear it.

"I've got to go."

She gathered some things, throwing them in the duffel bag. Things she'd need later. After drinking two glasses of water in the kitchen, she walked to the campervan door and stopped, her fingers on the handle. Laura turned back to look at the three people tied up in the bedroom. God, her shins were stinging.

She had to say something to these people. They had to know she wasn't the monster they thought she was. But there was no time. No time to tell them about the monster living under their roof. Not yet.

"I'm sorry you got caught up in this."

She opened the door. Felt a cool breeze rush into the living room. As if fleeing the night out there.

"Sit tight and stay quiet. It'll be over soon, I promise."

25

LAURA

Laura was back in the Ducato, sitting alongside Roz on the bedroom floor. Their masks were still on, the crude, carved-out features illuminated by the gloomy light from the kitchen. Their backs were tight against the wall.

They were watching Dirk.

He was still where Laura had left him earlier, sitting on the other side of the room, cross-legged, one wrist still cuffed to the foot of the bunk bed. There was an ugly red welt on his head. A souvenir from his encounter with Laura's rifle butt.

"My head's splitting," Dirk said.

Silence.

"Do you people hear me? It feels like you caved my skull in. I think I'm going to be sick."

"Do it," Laura said. "You're the one who'll be sitting in it."

He glared at her.

"I pissed myself," he said. "I pissed myself in front of my family."

If only you knew what was coming, Laura thought, staring at him through the vertically-slashed eyeholes. *That would be the least of your concerns.*

With sunrise, came payback. Dirk's happiness would live on only in memories. Just like it was for Laura.

"Fine. I'll be sick all over the floor."

"Shut it," Roz said. "Talking about being sick, are we? Well, I'm sick of the sound of your voice."

Dirk slumped backwards, falling against the bed. "What have you done with my family? Where did you take them?"

Laura recalled the way he'd watched her five years ago across the hotel room. The coldness of his eyes. Like she was a *thing*, a tool, a device to be squeezed. Something that existed only for the benefit of reviving his flatlining marriage. She only had to close her eyes to see him creeping over to the bed, shirt unbuttoned, reeking of smoke and whisky, with the iPad in hand.

Why should she feel bad about this?

Tonight's outcome was the inevitable conclusion to Dirk's twisted blackmail scheme. Five years later. Roz was right. There was no other way it could end.

Dirk's expression jumped between fearful and angry.

"Tell me! What have you done to my family?" It was comical the way he spat out the words, one rapid-fire breath fuelling the assault. A line of spit dribbled down his chin. His posture continued to wilt. "What do you want with us? Where's my family? What did you do to them?"

Roz slammed a fist off the floor. Laura felt the campervan shudder.

"God," Roz said. "Give me strength."

Roz's patience hung by a fraying thread. Laura didn't like

it. The comfort she'd felt at having Roz beside her was slipping away. Was Roz reliving her own past under the mask? Seeing her own demon cuffed to the bunk bed?

"Please," Dirk said, uncrossing his legs. He looked at his damp crotch. Then, the steel bracelet fastened around his wrist. His eyes were hopeless. "Please, tell me what you want."

"Do you love your family?" Laura asked. Her voice sounded cold and metallic.

"What? Of course I do."

"And you'd do anything for them?"

Dirk hesitated, as if sensing a trap.

"Yes."

"Good. There's something I want you to do. For *them*."

"What?"

"It's not for me. It's for your family."

"What is it?"

She reached into the back pocket of her jeans, pulling out a tiny plastic bag that she pinched in between her thumb and forefinger. Laura unclipped the bag. Lifted out a small sheet of blotting paper and held it aloft, showing it to Dirk.

"This."

His eyes narrowed in confusion.

"What is it?"

"Look at it, Dirk. You must have seen one of these before."

The blotting paper was cut into a dozen square tabs. There was a red love heart printed on the centre of each tab. Laura held the sheet higher, where it caught more of the pale light, allowing Dirk a better view. Then, she slowly peeled off one of the tabs, separating it from the sheet.

"This one's for you."

Dirk's face was blank. Then, his eyes lit up with fear. He sat up, shaking his head with ferocious speed. "N-n-no. Is t-t-that what I think it is?"

Roz laughed, as if the horror on Dirk's face was the greatest punchline ever.

"What do you think it is?"

Dirk stared at the tab like it was a grenade without the pin. "It's LSD."

"Give that man a prize," Roz said, slow clapping her hands.

Dirk recoiled from the object in Laura's fingers. His forehead glistened with sweat. "You want me to take that? Why?"

"You like being in control," Laura said. "That sort of thing matters to you, doesn't it? Everything has to be in order. Neat. Tidy. I know a control freak when I see one and I knew it the first time I laid eyes on you."

"What? You don't know me."

"Oh, but I do. You do silly things when your life gets out of control. You make silly choices that hurt other people. Don't you, Dirk? In fact, you'll do anything to get what you want. Doesn't matter who you step over to get it. Doesn't matter whose life you crush as long as you get yours."

She stared at him.

"Well?"

Dirk's voice was a whisper. Sounded like he was talking in church. "Do I know you?"

Laura stood up. Fixed the mask. She walked across the bedroom, kneeling down in front of Dirk. She held out the tab.

"Put it on your tongue. Let it dissolve."

Dirk's eyes widened. "I *can't*."

"We've got your family," Roz said. "Remember? Don't

want to cooperate with us? Okay then. Which one do you want us to shoot first, Dirky boy? Your wife? The boy? Let me guess – you'll pick the girl, won't you?"

Laura nodded. "Young women. They're expendable. Right?"

Dirk looked at her in confusion. He shook his head. Let out a loud sobbing noise. "Who are you people?" He shook his arm, rattling the handcuffs. Shook the bed. Gave up and slumped forward in exhaustion.

"Who are you?"

Laura leaned into him again. Offered Dirk the tab.

"It's a simple trade. A favour, look at it that way. I did you a favour once, don't you remember?"

She was smiling under the mask.

26

DIRK

Dirk looked at the tab. The smaller of the two women had placed it in the palm of his hand. There was no weight to the thing. Nothing at all. It was air. And yet, the thought of what it would do to him, to his mind, it made his stomach churn.

"I can't do this."

"Take it," the small woman said.

There was solid ground underneath Dirk, but it felt like he was falling into a deep hole. Without a parachute. Maybe it was the knock on the head. Maybe it was the fear. The shame of having pissed his pants in front of his wife. In front of his children. He put a hand on the floor to steady himself. There was no reasoning with these maniacs. Madwomen. The small one talked like she knew him. That didn't make sense. The big one just grunted every now and again, threatening violence.

He looked at the tab. Felt his guts churning with horror.

"P-p-please. Don't make...don't make me do this."

"Put the tab in your mouth," the small one said.

Dirk stared at it. Somehow, that love heart-shaped smudge on the front made it worse. A love heart? The ultimate symbol of goodness flipped upside down. Its red centre, a black hole waiting to devour him.

"No, I can't do this."

He offered the tab back to the masked woman, hoping that she'd take it away. Maybe she was bluffing. Maybe she was trying to scare him.

"I'm running out of patience with you," the small one said. "Put it on your tongue. The sooner you do, the sooner you'll see your family again. That's what you want, isn't it?"

Dirk's felt his legs shaking. How did she know? How could she know how much he feared this, the ultimate loss of control?

Acid. That's what the teenagers called LSD in the Amsterdam suburb where he'd grown up. The cool kids all took acid. The ones who played guitar, who wanted to be the next John Lennon. Acid, it was all about acid. Experimentation. Expansion of consciousness. Blah-blah-blah. Smelly longhairs disappearing into the local woods at the weekend, lighting fires, tripping out of their minds. Playing loud rock music. Dirk knew better than to take the shortcut through the woods at the weekend if he was going to the shops or the train station. His dad warned him about the hippies. About the druggies. People who'd never amount to anything in life, that's what the old man said. Their brains were fried eggs. Unable to cope with the real world, they'd be in a straitjacket before they were thirty. Pacing back and forth inside a padded cell, foaming at the mouth. LSD, the old man said, was the devil in a tie-dye t-shirt. Dirk despised the cool kids because his father despised them. Most of all, he despised them because they never invited him to join them, not once. Some of the girls who went into the woods with the hippies were gorgeous. Unbearably gorgeous. Maybe they'd loosen up on drugs. Let him touch them.

But no one invited him. Not ever. Not the stuttering weirdo.

"Put the tab on your tongue."

Dirk heard his father's voice. Like a distant bell ringing in the back of his mind.

Stinking hippies! Druggies. Foaming at the mouth.

The tab was heavier in his hand. People took these things for fun? He'd read somewhere that taking a super-human dose of psychedelics was the closest anyone could get to death without dying. Ego death, they called it.

Fun?

How was that fun?

Dirk wondered how the small woman could see through him with such ease. She seemed to be the one in charge, or at least, she was doing most of the talking. The big one was muscle. Never far from shouting or lashing out or pointing that rifle at Dirk's head. Had he met the smaller woman before? How did she know that losing control terrified him? Especially now, with a family and a good job and everything else he'd always wanted. His life had fallen into place. His was a story of triumph against the odds, of overcoming cruel, neglectful parents and a lonely childhood to become a success. He didn't want to lose control. He didn't want to lose his ego. Dirk *was* his ego. Without it, what was left?

"Do it," she said.

"N-n-no."

"Do it. That's the last time I'm going to ask nicely."

The warning sirens blared in Dirk's head. But what choice did he have? They'd taken his family. God knows where, but they had him by the balls. Dirk lowered his head, emitting a loud sobbing noise. Why was this happening? He was a good man. He didn't deserve this.

He wiped a tear off his cheek. Stared at the handcuff in defeat.

"Why? Please, tell me."

The woman fidgeted with the mask. Then she pointed at the tab in his palm. She spoke softly this time, like she was comforting him. "You want answers? You want to know why this is happening?"

Dirk nodded.

"You don't already know?"

"No."

"Then do it. Put the tab on your tongue. Go to Wonderland and I promise you, you'll find the answers you're looking for."

Dirk could still hear his father screaming. The old bastard's voice was swirling around inside his mind. The dead man that Hell didn't want, now using Dirk's mind as his own private afterlife. Telling him to man up. To stand up to these two bitches with sacks over their heads. They were only women under the masks. Probably didn't even know how to work those guns.

Before placing the tab on his tongue, he looked at the small one.

"Just tell me one thing. My family–"

"They're fine."

"How do I know that's true?" Dirk asked. "How do I know you're not just telling me what I want to hear?"

The woman's head tilted to the side, struck by curiosity. The mask slipped down her face, her eyes lost for a second before she fixed it.

She pointed at the tab.

"There's only one way to find out."

27

LAURA

Laura and Roz were standing outside in the pitch black. Taking a well-earned smoking break. This was their first since charging into Dirk's campervan about an hour ago.

Laura was grateful for the cigarette. Grateful for the break. Most of all, she was grateful for the opportunity to take off the mask. Let her face breathe, at least for a while. She leaned against the Ducato side door, lapping up the cool breeze.

They didn't talk. Just smoked. After the first cigarette, Laura lit two more. She handed the second one to Roz.

"Thanks," Roz said. She took the second cigarette, crushing the remains of the first under her foot. She picked it up, offered it to Laura. "For your box?"

"They've got bins around here."

Roz shrugged. Let the butt fall through her fingers. "How are you feeling, sweetheart? You're doing great in there."

Laura hesitated. "Thanks."

"Drink some water when you go back in. We're sweating like bastards under these masks."

"I will."

Roz did a sweep of the surroundings. A sea of black. Lights in the distance. "Quiet, isn't it?"

"Sure is," Laura said. "It's hard to believe that we're surrounded by holidaymakers on all sides, isn't it? Feels like there's no one else for miles."

Once again, they checked for lights. It was hard to stop thinking about it. About the possibility of one little busybody ruining everything. But, nothing. Not a squeak. There were no worried faces. No curtains twitching. No lights flickering on. And thank God, no wailing police siren in the distance.

"What's bugging you?" Roz asked.

"I can't stop thinking about them."

"About who?"

"Who? About those three innocent people tied up in the back of my van. That's who."

Roz shrugged. "Why?"

Laura's face wrinkled with disdain. "Shit, Roz. What if one of them needs to go to the toilet? I can just imagine that little boy in there, sitting in his own shit and piss. Trying to scream behind a gag. What if he's hyperventilating, his little heart beating like a panicked bird?"

"You want to call it off?" Roz asked.

"What sort of question is that?"

Roz blew smoke out hard. "Do you?"

"After all this? Of course not."

"Good. Because it's far too late in the day to back out."

"I'm not trying to back out," Laura said, sounding annoyed.

Roz nodded. Then she pointed towards the van. Her

voice shrinking to a whisper. "You think he's figured it out yet?"

"What?"

"That the LSD is fake."

"Don't know," Laura said, shrugging. "You?"

Roz smiled. Her teeth were yellowing from all the years of smoking. But she still had one hell of a smile. "No chance my darling. He's out of his head, I guarantee it. There's a lot of good evidence on psychedelic placebos out there. People who trip on fake drugs, at least when the conditions were right."

"Are the conditions right?" Laura asked.

"You saw how scared he was. His imagination is already working overtime thinking about what we did to his family."

Roz cackled to herself. She sucked on the cigarette, lighting the tip. The tobacco burned, a tiny orange sun in the dark.

Laura pointed across the caravan park. "Do you think I should go back? Check on them?"

"The wife and kids?"

The wife and kids. That's what Laura should still know them as. Instead, she had to go and learn their names. Diana, Isla, Joe. Big mistake. Dirk's name was the only one that mattered.

"Stop fretting," Roz said. "They're not going anywhere. They're tied up. As long as those knots are good, you have nothing to worry about."

"The knots are good."

"Then stop worrying."

"Jesus, Roz," Laura said, lifting her back off the van. Her shirt felt like it was glued to her skin with layers of cooling sweat. "There are two children in there. Gagged. Scared. What if something's happened?"

"Forget about it, hon. It's only going to get complicated if you start giving a shit."

"Easier said than done."

"Listen," Roz said. "You go over there, take their gags off and they'll do anything. They'll say anything. *I need to go to the bathroom. I'm asthmatic.* Whatever. And once they're up, they'll swing for the fences."

Laura hadn't told Roz about Diana's attack. How she'd already swung for the fences and missed. Barely. Laura wasn't sure why she hadn't told Roz. Was it because she didn't want to look incompetent? Or was she afraid that Roz would want to go over there and punish Diana? Discourage her from further bright ideas. Which, in order to do so effectively, meant punishing the kids.

"What if they do need to go to the toilet?" Laura asked.

"They can go where they are."

"Bloody hell. What if they need to be sick?"

Roz's face was as hard as rock. "They can swallow it."

"Fuck's sake Roz," Laura snapped. She paused. Glanced around the park for light or movement. Nothing – the sea of darkness was still. She brought the volume back down a notch. "They're gagged. They'll choke."

Roz's eyes flashed with anger. "Shit, will you give it a rest? Forget about the well-being of his fucking family, will you? Remember why we're doing this. Remember what he did to you."

"Yes," Laura said, not backing down. "What he did to *me*. Not you. *Me*."

She turned away. Focused on the glowing tip of the cigarette perched in between her fingers. A tiny oasis of light. It was hypnotic.

Roz put a hand on Laura's shoulders.

"You've got to keep hating him. Cling to it. Embrace it.

That's what'll get you through this shit. What we're doing here, yeah, it's fucked up. But where was justice when you deserved it back then? Who put you in this position? Who made Tommy think you were a slut? The sort of slut that cheated on him in cheap hotel rooms?"

"Him," Laura whispered.

"That's right. Think about that when it gets tough, hon. Think about *that*. Get angry because you deserve to be angry. You've got every right to do what you're doing tonight. What goes around comes around."

Roz's hard, unflinching stare seemed to float towards Laura.

"This doesn't end pretty, you know? What we're doing and what we're going to do, it's going to stay with you. You'll still have nightmares. But you'll also have justice."

"Roz," Laura said. "Are we really going to do this?"

"We are."

"There's no other way?"

The granite expression on Roz's face melted. A sad smile lingered for a second. Then she shook her head.

"They've seen your van. For all we know, one of them might have memorised the registration plate. We've been following them all day. Too many threads binding us, honey. We've started. We have to finish."

Laura felt hollow inside. She smoked the cigarette down to its filter. There was a cold, relentless churning sensation in her stomach that she couldn't shake. A faint ringing in her ears.

"What are we going to do with the bodies?"

"Make them disappear," Roz said in a matter-of-fact tone. "Lucky us, we're in the Highlands. Lots of places to make someone disappear around here. Don't worry sweetheart, I'm on it. We just need to start thinking about the time. Everything, and I mean *everything*, has to be done before the sun comes up."

Laura didn't understand how Roz could talk about these things in such a detached manner. Sounded like she was talking about dumping used furniture in a skip. They were talking about people. Three innocent people.

"Listen," Roz said. "If it makes you feel better, I'll go and check on the rest of the family. I could use the walk."

Laura nodded. "Thanks." She dug into her pocket, pulled out the key to the Grand California and handed it to Roz.

"Be careful."

"Don't worry," Roz said, taking the key. She blew a cloud of smoke into the night and set off. Turning around one last time. "What are you going to do while I'm gone?"

Laura was already on the step, reaching for the door handle.

"It's time me and Dirk had a little chat."

28

DIRK

Dirk stared at the wall. Waiting for the LSD to kick in.

How long had it been since the love heart dissolved on his tongue? Might have been ten minutes. Might have been an hour. Time didn't seem to matter anymore. What next? What was he going to see now that he'd been forced to become the sort of layabout that his father despised? Would he see his father in the campervan? Would the old man's head come floating across the bedroom to tell Dirk that he wasn't good enough? *God, please no.* Dirk's father had died fourteen years ago in Amsterdam, dropping stone dead of a heart attack in the back garden. His mother found him. The dog licking his dead face. Dirk never saw the body. Still, he could imagine his father's face as it lay there on the grass, stiffening with rigor mortis. The look of eternal disappointment. Eyes that would follow his son forever.

Dirk could feel the drug seeping into his system. A chemical invasion. Poisoning his mind. So far, it wasn't that bad. He'd giggled, mostly out of nerves. That was the deception. That was the drug, making him feel good while turning him inside out.

Junkie! Druggie!

The two masked women had stepped outside. Were they gone? Was the ordeal over now that they'd forced the LSD into him?

He looked around the bedroom. All the microscopic details, everything on the walls and floor were so much bigger than they'd been before. Insignificant specks, stains, blemishes, all transformed into jaw-dropping tapestries. The beautiful world inside the Fiat Ducato, so mundane before, had come into sharper focus.

This stuff is messing with my head.

"How's it going Dirk?"

Dirk flinched at the sound of the woman's voice. It came out of nowhere. Was it real? He jerked the arm that was still cuffed to the bed. Felt a sharp pinch on his wrist. Heard a loud metallic rattle that snapped at his ears.

"What the–?"

He blinked hard. Looked across the bedroom. There she was, the smaller of the two women. But her mask was off. She was a blue-headed blur, her back pressed against the wall. Face slightly out of focus.

"Are you okay?" she asked.

"Are you real?"

She nodded.

"Do you remember me?"

"You're the one in the Grand California," Dirk said. "You nearly ran over Joe and Isla this morning. I saw you at the monument."

The woman nodded again. "But that's not who I am. So, I'll ask you again. Do you remember me?"

Dirk exploded with nervous laughter. He clamped a hand over his mouth to contain it. "W-w-what did you say?"

"You heard."

He pointed a finger at her. "You're the Devil."

The blue-headed creature made a scraping noise as she moved closer. Sounded like sharp claws raking the floor. There was a coldness to her voice. "I'm not. But as far as you're concerned, I might as well be."

"Why? Because my children ran in front of your van?"

"You're not seeing the big picture, Dirk. This isn't about what happened at Skiach."

"Then, what's it about?"

"I want you to recognise me."

Dirk blinked hard again. A rainbow of impossible colours flooded his vision. *My God*, he thought. *I'm tripping.*

"Look at me," she said.

He did. This time, Dirk really looked. Sure enough, there was something familiar about the woman's face. Dirk's head leaned in. He shimmied his backside along the floor, trying to get a better look. As he moved, the light trickling in from the kitchen shimmered. Dirk gasped, as if some kind of major celestial event had just happened.

He turned back to the woman.

"You're pretty."

"Thank you. Not as pretty as I used to be though, am I?"

Dirk's face creased up. He shrank backwards, recoiling from the sound of her voice. His back slammed against the ladder on the bunk bed. "No, I don't know you."

"You know me."

"I don't."

He gasped again. To his horror, the woman was laughing. Her face, a blue-haired skull, its macabre grin inching closer across the bedroom. She spoke louder. An explosion of anger distorting her voice.

"Who am I?"

Dirk shook his head. "No, no, no."

"Who am I, Dirk?"

He paused. For a moment, he was floating above his body. Watching the scene below from the detached vantage point of the ceiling. From up there, it was clear. Everything made perfect sense. Of course. It was her. It was *her*. The truth crashed into Dirk like an Earth-sized wrecking ball. He was back on the floor now. Cuffed to the bed. He made a whimpering noise as he realised for the first time what was happening here. Buried his face deep in his free hand, not able to look at her.

"No!"

The cold metal voice sounded like it was inside his head.

"Who am I? Say it."

There was a long silence before Dirk took his hand away from his face. He looked at the blue monster. "Y-y-you're the Don't Drink Girl."

The woman sat there, looking at Dirk like he was a grotesque exhibit in a jar.

"It's you," he said. "Isn't it?"

She gave a slight nod. "What's my real name? What name did I have back then?"

"W-w-what?"

"It's a simple question. What's my name, Dirk? The one that's on my birth certificate. I'll give you a hint. It's not Don't Drink Girl."

Dirk's tongue was mush in his mouth. His mind was shrivelling up into a fried egg, just like his father told him it would. He was losing the ability to form words and string coherent sentences together.

"D-d-don't know."

The woman stood up. The floor creaked as she took a step closer.

Looking at her, Dirk recalled the way she'd been back then. He hadn't forgotten that much at least. Long blonde hair, milky-white skin and good dress sense. Much prettier than she was now. She'd really let herself go. No makeup. She was too skinny. Wearing rags that could barely be called clothes. One thing was for sure. If she'd climbed into the back of his car looking like that five years ago, Dirk wouldn't have touched her with a bargepole.

"I lost everything because of you," she said. "And you can't even remember my name?"

"S-s-sorry."

"My fiancée dumped me. I lost my home, my dog, my parents, all my friends and my dream job. Because of you. What you did. Your footage was good, Dirk. It was so good it fooled everyone. They looked at me like I was someone else. A liar and a cheat. Can you imagine what that feels like? And yet here you are, doing well for yourself. A real happy chappy. Got that nice family you always wanted, eh?"

"You've been watching me?"

"Bet you wish you'd gone somewhere else for breakfast, eh?"

Dirk felt the cold dread pooling in his stomach. He touched his face. It felt spongy. "I don't like this. When will this stuff wear off?"

She shrugged. "Maybe never. They say once it's in your system, it never leaves."

Dirk could still hear his father's voice roaring in his head. Good old Ruben De Vries. He wasn't going anywhere. "Please, make it stop. I've had enough."

The woman convulsed with laughter. It sounded like an

electric drill in Dirk's mind. "Wow! Your pupils are massive, Dirk. I think maybe we've fucked up. Given you too much. And this is your first time taking it too, right? Whoops. I don't even know if you'll survive that sort of dosage."

"STOP!"

She knelt down beside him.

"It's not nice being drugged against your will, is it?"

"No."

"No, it's not. Trust me, I understand. I've been there. I know how vulnerable you must feel right now, not having the slightest bit of control over any of this."

Dirk lunged at the woman. But she was too quick, slipping out of range as if she'd seen the whole thing coming. She straightened back up. Towered over him. Eyes shimmering in silent fury.

"I'm sorry," he said, burying his face in his hand again. He wanted to drown there. But he looked up. "Please f-f-forgive me. I'm s-s-sorry."

She walked away. Stopped in the doorway. Turned around to face him, a dark silhouette with no expression.

"About your wife and kids," she said in a quiet voice. "You didn't really think I was going to let them go, did you?"

29

LAURA

Laura stepped outside, wiping the sweat off her forehead. She closed the campervan door behind her.

"Fuck."

She was shaking. She was burning up. And yet, despite all the emotion, the big reveal had been a strangely anti-climactic sensation. The twisted bastard thought he was tripping in there. He'd been distracted. Laura wanted more. More than what she got from him.

There was still plenty of time.

"No turning back now," she whispered to herself.

She felt the dryness of her throat. It was scalding. Burning up like a desert in the hot sun. Laura could hear Dirk sobbing from the bedroom. When she left him, he was face down on the floor, begging for mercy.

Laura held all the cards. She was in complete control of this man and yet she wasn't enjoying any of it. She was enduring it. Hell on earth. An out-of-control rollercoaster ride, no way to get off. Where was the payoff? Dirk got happiness in return for his sins. What would Laura get when it was all over?

"Everything okay?"

Roz's boots crunched off the grass as she emerged from the darkness. Her stride was long and relaxed. "How's he doing in there?"

"Crying his eyes out."

"Poor baby."

"How are the others?" Laura asked.

"They're fine," Roz said. "I told you, didn't I? No one's sitting in their bodily fluids or anyone else's for that matter, so you can relax. They're pretty calm, all things considered."

"Calm? Are you serious?"

"I am."

Laura rolled up the sleeves of her shirt. Her arms were soaked with sweat. She took a series of slow, deep breaths. "Roz–"

"I know what you're going to say," Roz said, jumping in. "It's getting harder. But you've got this. Trust me, you'll only hate yourself if you run away again."

"Will I?"

"Hated yourself after Fyrish, didn't you?"

"What if I can't do it?" Laura asked. "When the time comes..."

Roz wrapped an arm around Laura's shoulder. Gave her a squeeze. "We've been through this, haven't we?"

"But–"

"Shhh."

Roz put a finger to her lips. Her stern expression was a door slamming in the face of Laura's ongoing concern. "You're my best friend and I love you. That's why I'm here. I'm putting myself at risk just being here, you know?"

"I know that."

"Good. I'm not going to let you make another mistake."

They listened to Dirk weeping inside the van. Talking to himself, muttering a nonsensical apology to someone. Laura glanced around the caravan park. Any louder and she'd have to go in and gag him. That wouldn't be fun, but they had to keep him quiet. There was always a chance that someone would wake up. A light would go on. A face would appear at the window. A knock on the door.

Is everything alright?

"He's not a nice family man," Roz said, eyes burning with intensity. "Men like him, they want you to think they're the bee's knees. Clean-cut on the outside. Mummy's boys. They smile for the cameras, pay for the meal and say all the right things at the right time, just enough to furnish their own bullshit myth. They put out a nice, wholesome image. And they believe in it. They're clever, but they're not nice men. Remember that sweetheart. All we're doing tonight is swatting a big fly."

She reached for the door. Looked up at the sky, nodding to herself.

"We'd better get moving. Not long till dawn."

PART III

THE LONG NIGHT

30

DIRK

Dirk was cold. His mind, as gooey as sludge. He was outside. He was walking. Felt like he was trying to pull himself out of a dream that wasn't ready to end.

Something scratched his arm. Looking up, he saw a sharp, hooked branch hanging down from the outline of a gigantic tree. It was reaching for him. *Scratch*. Another one, raking his skin like a claw. Dirk winced. He walked faster, aware that something heavy was bumping against his leg. *Thump, thump, thump*. He looked down. It was so dark he couldn't see much of anything.

He stopped. Looked around, his fast-blinking eyes trying to penetrate the wall of darkness that closed in on all sides. Only the outline of tall, stooped shapes was visible. Trees. Everywhere. All of them grabbing at him.

The woods. That's right. He was in the woods.

What was he doing here?

Bump.

Dirk had a buzz saw headache, splitting his skull in two. He staggered forward, a blind man, using his arms for balance and to ward off any potential obstacles.

He heard the rattle of the handcuffs. The cold, metallic clink taunting his efforts to make sense of things. He tried to speak, but his voice was muffled behind a gag.

He stopped.

Flash memories of how he ended up in the woods. Tripping in the bedroom, cuffed to the bunk bed. The big woman storming in, raising the rifle over her head and bringing the butt down on his skull. Dirk had blacked out. He woke up while the two women were carrying him out of the campervan. His scream lost behind the gag. He recalled the bitter taste of tape. They carried him across the park in silence. One had his arms, the other held his legs. A sloppy transport job, their frantic breath in his ears. Clearly, he was heavier than they'd been expecting.

Then, he was going into another campervan. The Grand California.

Another knock on the head.

Blackness.

Waking up, the van jerking along a bumpy road. Handcuffed. Semi-conscious, his head leaning against the cold glass window. The blue-haired woman sat beside Dirk in silence. No more masks. Where were they taking him? Looking outside, he saw billions of stars. The smallness he felt in their presence was comforting. What did it matter? What did any of it matter in the grand scheme of things?

Diana. Isla. Joe.

Panic.

Where were they?

The van raced over winding roads and Dirk's stomach

lurched with each and every turn. The wooziness was too much. He blacked out. Woke up as the California screeched to a stop. The engine was turned off and the sudden silence was unbearably loud. The doors were opened. Dirk felt hands all over him again, grabbing and pulling. He was bundled outside. That's when he lost consciousness yet again, not sure if he'd ever wake up.

Now, here he was. Trudging through the woods. It felt like he'd been walking for hours. What time was it? Why couldn't he think straight?

Was it the drugs? The blows to the head?

He couldn't even scream.

A mild breeze fluttered against his face. He looked up and the vast night sky pressed down harder. An ocean of black. The stars burned brighter, billions of eyes watching him. He skipped forward on unsteady feet, like a child learning how to walk. *Bump.* He looked around, saw nothing but the trees and their grabbing limbs. *Bump.* Felt like he was hitting his leg off dead stumps. When he got closer, he saw faces carved into the trees. Ancient faces that he'd seen before.

He'd walked through the woods already tonight. Hadn't he?

Dirk kept walking. His feet, sinking into the soft ground. *Bump.*

A light up ahead! Two glorious suns, shimmering in the distance. And with it, a faint purring that sounded a lot like an idling car. The road. Couldn't be that far. Dirk felt a rush of sudden excitement at this discovery. He'd follow the light. Walk to the road and signal for help. Then, he'd get after these women. He'd get his family back.

He shuffled forwards. Trying to keep his balance.

Bump.

Dirk kept his eyes on the headlights. He was terrified that the vehicle would move on before he could get to it. Maybe the headlights were just a mirage. A symptom of the damage he'd taken to the skull. Could be the drugs.

Oh God, he thought. *Let this be over.*

It felt like there was a giant python wrapping its thick coils around his body. With every inhalation, the snake squeezed tighter. Still, he hurried along, his spongy limbs drowning in the forest floor.

Bump.

Thank God for the stars.

He plodded on, short careful strides leading him to the road. What he hoped was the road. The way home.

Bump.

Another scream lost behind the gag. He had to stay calm. Breathe through the nose.

Why did it feel like he was being watched?

The handcuffs rattled. His footsteps, ragged and heavy. But he didn't go down, *wouldn't* go down. Didn't matter if Dirk's legs got bruised and scraped and chopped to ribbons. If he tripped, he'd get up. If he couldn't walk, he'd crawl. All that mattered was getting out of these woods and finding his family. Getting even with that blue-haired bitch.

C'mon, he urged himself.

Dirk covered ten good metres. Almost a sprint. Then he stopped. His blood ran cold. He'd touched something with his fingertips after lowering his arms to shake off the numb. Something hot and sticky, something that was clinging to his thigh.

He waddled forward.

Bump. Bump. Bump.

He wasn't bumping into something that belonged in the

woods. Not tree stumps, branches or anything else. This thing. It was on his leg.

He looked down. Strained his eyes. Reached his cuffed arms towards the thing and that's when he touched it. The jolt of terror almost knocked him off his feet.

Hair.

Dirk screamed behind the gag. The sound had nowhere to go and he swallowed it, recycling the terror. He was losing his mind. Sliding into insanity.

There was no mistaking it. It was Diana's hair.

Her severed head was tied to his leg.

Bump. Bump. Bump.

Dirk, still screaming, burst into a ferocious sprint. He fell over seconds later, crash-landing on a pile of branches and fallen leaves. Something scratched his cheek. A hot, stinging pain filled his head. As he went down, he felt his wife's head thumping against the leg.

She was resting on his thigh.

Another gagged scream.

This was Diana's terrible fate. But where were the kids? Had the masked bitches killed and mutilated them too? Children for God's sake, children! His family. Gone. He'd waited so long for a family and now they were dead, all because of the blue-haired monster's petty desire for vengeance.

Dirk's body trembled. He felt an explosion of rage surging up inside.

I'll show you vengeance, he thought.

They'd left him alive. That was their first mistake. Now, Dirk had to reach the light on the road. He had to get out of here.

He tried to yell behind the gag.

"Stop! Please stop."

It came out a gargled mess.

But he was on his feet. Dirk found an extra gear, running wild and ape-like towards the road with Diana's head slapping off his leg. He heard her voice, a shrill roar that came not just from his leg, but also from the ancient faces carved into the trees. It sounded like the entire forest was screaming at him.

DIRK! Look at what she did to me. This is your fault. I knew you were a mistake. Why the hell did I marry such a pathetic loser?

Where are my children?

Dirk grimaced at the wet squelching noise on his leg. But he was almost out. The headlights were no more than fifteen metres away on what appeared to be a single-track road that sliced its way through the woodland.

He tried to yell. Tried to wave his arms in the air, the cuffs throwing him off balance.

They had to see him. With any luck, it was a group of holidaymakers. They'd get a shock but they'd take him to the nearest police station. He'd raise the alarm. The blue-haired bitch, along with her giant accomplice, would spend the rest of their lives in prison, rotting behind bars.

Now that he was on the road, he ran like a sprinter, all guns blazing. It felt like the forest was chasing him. Like it wanted him back. He imagined cold hands grabbing at his hair. At his arms. Legs. Malicious forces, intent on keeping Dirk trapped in the dark forever. The head bumped against his leg. He couldn't look at it. Couldn't bear to think about what would happen next. When he was in the light. The cloudiness of death in her eyes. Her beautiful eyes.

No, he wouldn't look. Wouldn't ever look. That's not how he'd remember her.

Dirk ran onto the dirt track. Every step felt like it was along the edge of a tall cliff. One with a steep drop.

With arms aloft, he waved down the blinding set of headlights.

Thank God, he thought.

They'd seen him.

The car was rolling towards him.

31

DIRK

Thank you, Dirk thought, watching the headlights approach.

Tyres crunched over the narrow track. The gravel underneath was spat out in all directions. Dirk narrowed his eyes against the fierce glare of headlights.

He staggered up the narrow incline, one step at a time. Breathing hard. Doing his best not to catch a glimpse of Diana's head. The constant sensation of her skull drumming on the outside of his leg was excruciating.

He stopped as the vehicle met him in the middle of the road.

Dirk dropped to his knees. Then, he saw it. His eyes bulged with horror.

It wasn't a car. It was a campervan.

The Grand California screeched to a sudden stop. Smoke billowed out of the exhaust pipe. It shuddered as the people inside waited for Dirk to make his move.

Dirk knew that screaming from behind the gag was of no use. He turned around. Pumped his exhausted arms and legs, fuelled by raw panic. His skin burned. He took off down the slight incline that wound its way to the left. Lungs on fire. The mangled head of his wife slapped off his leg in quick time.

The van doors opened. Dirk heard footsteps on the track. Someone breaking into a full-on sprint behind him. Sounded like a gazelle on his heels. When Dirk finally looked over his shoulder, he saw the blue headed monster closing the gap with ease. Her eyes were cruel and focused. There was something in her hand.

Dirk turned his head back. Immediately lost balance and tripped. He went down, just as the woman caught up with him. He landed on his back, watching as the blue-haired monster raised her arm back over her shoulder. The attack came down hard and fast. Something metal hit the top of Dirk's head. *Whack*. A flurry of bright lights. The woods across the road were spinning at a hundred miles per hour. She hit him again.

This happened before, Dirk thought. *It's happened before.*

They'd caught him. Hit him. So many times.

Strong arms locked around his waist. Looking up, Dirk saw the giant grinning at him. No mask. Black eyes. Terrifying, demonic features. They sat him up. Took a hold of his arms and legs and dragged him back into the woods.

32

LAURA

They'd just put Dirk back in Camore Wood for the fifth time. He was probably concussed. Five times and still he didn't understand what was going on. Still, he kept emerging from the woods every fifteen minutes or so, full of hope, running towards the California's headlights like they were his salvation. Each time, a little slower. His posture more stooped. A moth doomed to chase the flames until he burned.

Laura glanced at Roz. They'd done terrible things tonight.

Was she as bad as Dirk?

Worse?

Despite their crimes, Roz was still unflappable. She smoked in the passenger seat, her thick arm hanging out of the rolled-down window. Letting the air on her skin. She was humming a tune under her breath. 'Daydream Believer'.

Her shirt was speckled with blood.

Whatever Laura had feared about Roz's descent into darkness, it had come to pass. And Roz showed no signs of slowing down, even as dawn approached. This was *Laura's* revenge or at least it had been. Roz had taken over. This was Roz's revenge and Laura couldn't forget that its terrible, bloody climax was fast approaching.

Laura was spent. She was sick of running Dirk down at the side of the road. Sick of hitting him over the head with a crowbar. Sick of hauling him back into the woods to resume his Sisyphean punishment. On and on it went. Who was really punishing who here? She was sick of waiting in the car with the lights on full beam, luring him out.

Exhaustion pulled her down into the murky depths. She was dehydrated and there was little to zero food in her stomach. It felt like years since she'd slept.

The thought felt blasphemous. But it was there. Laura willed Dirk to escape this time. To get away, to bring this hunt to an end. It would've been easy too, if only the bastard's mind could right itself. He could walk the other way. Go into Camore Wood and walk away from the road, venture into darkness and take his chances. But he kept coming back, drawn to the California's headlights. To the thought of rescue.

Was it the two children? Was that what kept bringing him back?

Was he even thinking at all?

Laura wanted to go back to the services. Back to the services in Skiach, yesterday morning. Go back to standing in line with her food tray. Look the other way, even knowing that Dirk was in the restaurant. Fuck him. Nothing would bring her old life back. Certainly not the shit they'd been doing all night. Laura didn't even want her old life back. This wasn't so bad. A simple life in the Highlands, making art and taking it on the road. Less clutter. Less busyness.

They watched through the windscreen. Waiting for him to appear. Waiting for that strange walk to reveal itself yet again. Like the man's limbs were made of jelly. If his brain was still mush, then he'd run to them. Crying for help behind the tape. Like he'd done so many times tonight. And they'd go to him.

With the crowbar.

Cool air blew out of the vents. Laura glanced up and down the road, wondering if anyone else, tourists or locals, would show up before this thing was over. Before the dawn. That was all they needed. People. Questions.

Laura looked at her friend's rifle, propped up on the footrest. The cigarette smoke in the van was a neverending cloud that made her feel nauseated. The old Laura had always hated it when people smoked back in Glasgow. How had she become one of those people?

"If he gets lost," Roz said, pointing at the woods, "we'll have to go in there after him."

"Right."

"Nope. Wait a second. Is that–?"

Roz slapped a hand off her thigh, then burst into a fit of laughter. "Thank God, we don't have to put on our running shoes just yet. There he is. See him? Coming back to his two mummies like a good boy."

"Where?"

"Look down there. Same place as last time. I think he's found a second wind. Coming out a little faster, don't you think?"

Laura stared through the windscreen. The darkness had faded, just enough for her to see the hunched figure of Dirk still chasing the headlights. His feet scraped off the gravel.

All he could do was shuffle. Inch by agonising inch. There was something about the way he moved, Laura thought, something that didn't seem human anymore.

Roz picked up the crowbar. "Look at him. Even with a concussion, you'd think enough was enough."

Laura looked at the crowbar in Roz's hand.

"Fuck this."

"What's up, hon?" Roz asked.

Laura didn't answer. She pushed the driver's side door open, jumping out onto the road. She walked over to Dirk. His eyes widened in terror at her approach. In one foul swoop, Laura pulled the tape off his mouth. There was a loud ripping noise. Sounded like she'd taken half his face off along with the tape.

Dirk let out a monstrous gasp. He wobbled backwards, then dropped to his knees. He pointed at the head stuck to his leg. Looking away from it.

"T-t-take it off! Take it off!"

His hands were clasped.

"Please...take...it off."

Laura squatted down beside him. Where was the anger? Where was the hate she needed? She looked deep into his eyes. Two black holes, shimmering with madness. Far removed from the cold indifference she'd encountered in him five years ago.

"P-p-please take it off," he said, his arm shaking.

Laura heard thunderous footsteps at her back. The giant figure of Roz appeared at the side of the road. She gave Laura a bewildered look, then, snatched the tape out of her hand and pressed it back over Dirk's mouth. She pushed hard at the sides, making sure it stayed in place.

Dirk tried to scream. Roz lashed out, hitting him on the shoulder with the crowbar she'd brought with her. He toppled over onto the gravel. She grabbed his arm. Nodded towards Camore Wood.

"Let's go."

Laura stood up. Shook her head.

Roz frowned. Kept a hold of Dirk's arm. "Excuse me?"

"I've had enough of this shit. The sun's coming up and we need to go."

"Are you serious?"

Laura nodded. "I'm serious."

Roz went back, like she'd been pushed. "Hon, we've got work to do. There's a mess that we both made. And it needs cleaning up."

Dirk was crying on the road. His body flopped to one side while Roz held his arm aloft. He looked like an oversized doll, ripe for the scrapyard.

Roz dragged Dirk back towards the woods. Singing 'Daydream Believer' at the top of her voice, as if she wanted to wake up the world.

"One more lap, eh Dirky boy? Let's see if you figure it out this time."

Roz didn't answer. Laura watched as she disappeared into the jaws of Camore Wood with Dirk. It was several minutes before Roz reappeared and the two women walked back to the van in silence. Roz handed Laura the crowbar while she wiped the dirt off her hands. They reached the Grand California, Roz walking around the back. She tapped the rear doors.

"Okay hon, you win."

"I win?"

"Yep."

"What do you mean?" Laura asked.

"It is getting a little tedious, isn't it? Waiting for Dirk to come back out. And you're right, we don't have long before daylight."

"You mean it's over?"

"It will be," Roz said. "Just one more thing to take care of first. You know what I mean, don't you sweetie?"

Laura swallowed back the burning in her throat.

"No."

"Yes you do."

"Let's call it a night, Roz. What do you say? We've done enough to them, haven't we?"

Roz shook her head. "We've done plenty, but we haven't done enough to leave ourselves in the clear. That's why we need to get rid of the witnesses. It's nothing personal. It's just cleaner this way."

"Fuck that."

Roz stepped forward. The look in her eyes. It was the same shimmering madness she'd seen in Dirk's moments earlier.

"We spoke about this, didn't we?"

"Roz," Laura said, lowering her voice. She could feel daylight falling like a giant net over her head. "I'm backing out. I'm not going to kill children for the likes of him. That wasn't me who agreed to your plan. Me? I'm the one who ran from Dirk at Fyrish. It wasn't cowardice. It was smart. I don't give a fuck about him anymore. He's not worth my time."

Roz remained still. "You're letting them go?"

"Yes."

"The fuck we are."

Roz grabbed the crowbar out of Laura's hand. She swung it like a bat, smashing it off the back of the campervan. It sounded like a clap of thunder. Laura heard muffled squeals of terror from the children tied up inside the van.

"He'll come back," Roz said, pointing to the woods. She was breathing heavy. Chest rising and falling. "And this time, he's going to watch us blowing their heads off. One little head at a time. Pop! Bang! And afterwards, he lives with the grief. Except he can't. Bingo. He's in the madhouse. And that's your revenge."

"It's *your* revenge, Roz."

Laura heard a gargled sob inside the van. Sounded like the boy.

"Fuck them," Roz barked. Then she leaned closer to Laura. Her voice an ecstatic whisper. "He'll think about you every day. When he wakes up in his padded cell, foaming at the mouth, your face will be the first thing he sees. You'll haunt him. You'll live in his dreams, you'll be everywhere he looks. The last thing he sees at night when they turn off the lights. He's not a nice family man. These people deserve what they get."

"It's gone too far," Laura said.

"I'm sorry you feel that way," Roz said, backing off. She went to the passenger side door, came back with two rifles. She handed one to Laura. "This *is* happening. And we're going to make him watch."

33

DIRK

Tell me everything Dirk. Tell me what you did to that woman?

"Stop it," Dirk said. The words didn't come out right behind the gag. He repeated them anyway, a series of stifled grunts. "*Stuppit, stuppit, stuppit.*"

What did you do to that woman with the blue hair? What did you do to make her come after us like this? What aren't you telling me Dirk?

Dirk wasn't sure when Diana's head started talking to him. It didn't matter when because the head *was* talking to him. Rapid-fire questions. Spitting them out. Decapitated heads didn't need to pause for breath. Diana wasn't going to shut up. She would talk and talk and talk. And why should she shut up? This was all Dirk's fault. Everything that happened, it was on him. She died because of Dirk's desperation five years ago. Her kids would probably die too, if they weren't already dead. It was only right that she should haunt him.

I'm sorry, he thought.

He was down on all fours, crawling through the forest like a frightened animal. His hands were covered in dirt and scratches.

The headlights on the road were bad. He knew that now. No salvation there. Maybe, despite the sound of his dead wife's voice blaring in his ear, Dirk's head was beginning to clear of the LSD fog. Not to mention all the hits he'd taken on the head. He wasn't fooled anymore. Lights bad. Road bad.

Go the other way.

What about Isla you bastard? What about Joe? Have you forgotten about our children you snivelling coward? Well, they're really MY children, aren't they? They were always MY children. Your own blood children don't want to know you. They call Amir Dad now, don't they? Smart kids. Why don't your kids want anything to do with you? What don't I know about you? Did you really tell me the full story about what happened with Court? What did you do to HER? What did you do to all these women?

Dirk crawled over a bed of fallen branches. He gasped for air. Winced at the sensation of a thousand tiny spear tips piercing the skin on his hands. At the same time, his wife's rotting head pressed against his leg.

DIRK!

A sudden lurching sensation in his stomach forced him to a dead stop.

He threw up. Looked down at the mess he'd made. He could see some of the chips he'd eaten at Dornoch Beach in the warm slop covering his hands.

Disgusting, he thought, although the warmth of the vomit wasn't so bad. Besides, throwing up made him feel better. His head was definitely clearing. But he wouldn't look into the eyes of his dead wife. Her face, frozen in a look of accusation. Disgust. Regret. The severed neck. The hair. And worst of all, her beautiful face.

Dirk couldn't bear that.

Look at me. Coward.

He shook his head. Wiped his hands dry on the ground. Then, he was back on his feet, staggering forwards, bracing himself for another fall. He didn't trust his body, especially his legs.

Bump.

I always knew there was something off about you. Look what she did to me! Look at the state of me! I'm a mother. I've got two children. What the hell are you doing? Are you running away from that van? Away from Joe and Isla when they need you the most?

Dirk stopped.

He *was* running away from the road. Away from his children.

Turn around for God's sake you pathetic bastard. Go get the children before something terrible happens. Do the right thing for once in your life.

Dirk started walking, trying to ignore the voice of his dead wife. But she was there with him, every step of the way, her voice echoing from all around the woods. She was in the carved faces, making their wooden lips move. Making their eyes follow him. Her voice turned the gentle breeze into a whip.

Don't you dare abandon my children!

"Fine!" Dirk yelled, hands clamped tight over his ears. He squeezed hard, like his head was a giant zit to be popped. Leaned his shoulder up against the nearest tree, desperately trying to catch his breath. The outer bark was rough. He stayed there for a minute, then turned back towards the road. Sure enough, the headlights were still there. Bait.

Luring him out. He could hear the engine. Could feel them waiting.

Don't leave my children.

Dirk nodded, then walked towards the light, a strange and sudden euphoria washing over him.

"I won't."

I'm a good man, he thought.

He held his head high. Saw the tip of a golden light creeping over the edge of the horizon. It was the beginning of a sunrise he thought he'd never see. Something that Diana would never see.

Slowly, he reached down and began stroking her hair.

"I'll save them."

Hurry Dirk. Hurry for God's sake.

34

LAURA

Laura could hear Dirk's raking footsteps spilling out of Camore Wood. He was talking to himself. From afar, it sounded like gibberish.

Roz looked towards the woods. Dead-eyed. Rifle in hand.

"We're almost done."

Laura did a quick scan of the road, still worried about people showing up. Especially now that it was getting lighter. The skies were clear. Pink, golden light speckled the horizon. The scout of dawn, chiselling at the fading gloom of last night. There had to be people camping overnight in one of the allocated campsites nearby. Some of them would be getting up soon. An early morning walk. A run. There were houses in the vicinity too, scattered along the main road. Less than a mile away. As for now, the Grand California was tucked out of sight on the single-track. But there would be no escaping the dawn.

She glanced at her phone.

4.52am.

Laura had been awake for twenty-four hours straight. She'd barely eaten. Her last drink of water was well over an hour ago. She was running on empty. Still smoking, even though the cigarette supply was almost gone. Her skin and clothes reeked of stale cigarettes. Just like Dirk in that hotel room five years ago.

"Let's get them out, shall we?"

Roz reached for the door handle. She pulled the double doors open and it made a tired, groaning noise. Like it had been disturbed.

Laura took a step closer. She didn't want to look inside that door-shaped black hole at the back of the campervan, but she had to. She heard a noise first. The faint, staccato whimpering of gagged children. It spilled out. Grew louder. The frantic wriggling on the bed. Then, she saw them. Isla and Joe huddled together, sitting back-to-back. Tied up, eyes bulging with fear and exhaustion as they stared out at their captors.

Fuck, Laura thought.

"We're bringing you out," Roz said. She spoke in a gentle voice. The voice of a stranger trying to convince Isla and Joe that, despite everything that had happened, she was a friend. "It's over. Okay? Your dad's on his way. Don't worry, nobody's going to hurt you."

Laura couldn't stomach that. This lying to children in the last moments of their lives, deceiving them right up until the very end, it felt as bad as anything they'd done that night. And they'd done some twisted shit.

She barged past Roz, slamming the van doors shut. Laura spun around, pinning her back against it. Arms spread out to the sides.

"No."

"What the hell are you doing?" Roz asked. She took a step towards Laura, rifle in hand. "You see that sunlight poking its head above the horizon, don't you? We don't have time to discuss this *again*. I told you, we're in it to deep."

"Roz, this was a mistake. *My* mistake. I shouldn't have called you."

"But you did. We made a mess and now we have to clean it up."

Laura shook her head. She looked at the Remington in Roz's hand. The barrel slowly swinging its way upwards in the big woman's calloused grip. Laura's own rifle was still lowered at the side. She didn't know her next move. Was she supposed to bring it into play? Was this a standoff? Is that what their friendship had come to?

"This isn't about Dirk anymore," she said. "It's not about what happened to me. Is it?"

Roz's eyes flashed with anger. "What's that supposed to mean?"

"Nobody murders innocent children as a favour. This is about what you went through in London. It's about getting back at *him* all over again. But Dirk's not the man you hate. He's not Darryl."

The name caused Roz to flinch. Her eyes turned over. It was subtle, but Laura saw it.

"Laura, they're all the same."

Roz's voice was flat. Distant.

"Daryll's dead. Remember? I know, it's not enough. One time. It'll never be enough to make up for what he did. But you got him. You *killed* him."

"They're all the same," Roz said.

"Roz, killing children isn't going to fix people like us. Some things break and they stay broken. We just have to live with it."

There was a smile on Roz's face. For a second, Laura thought she'd reached her. Then, Roz's eyes clouded over.

"I get it sweetheart. You're nervous."

"Not nervous," Laura said. "Finished."

Roz shook her head. It might as well have been a stranger standing in front of Laura on that quiet stretch of road beside the woods. A dark butterfly had emerged from the cocoon of her laid-back friend. The friend she relied on for keeping her sane, the one she shot beer cans with at the back of the old farmhouse. The one she smoked weed with. Drank tea with, while watching the sunrise. Roz was the safety net, the person who'd caught Laura so many times over the years. Laura didn't know if she could still catch Roz. Or if she'd already landed.

"Roz, you're not thinking straight."

"I'm the *only* one thinking straight," Roz said. "I don't want this mess coming back on us. And if we stop now, this *will* come back on us. That means a knock on the door, a dawn raid on my farmhouse. On your van. We have to finish what we started. You wanted revenge, hon. Well, here you go. Told you it was ugly."

Laura's voice cracked. "Roz, I can't–"

"We're running out of time, sweetie."

Laura took her back off the van. She staggered a few paces down the road. Felt like she was having a dizzy spell.

"You okay, hon?"

"Fine."

"Don't worry," Roz said, putting a hand on Laura's shoulder. "This is what you called me for. To get us over the finish line. Look, they won't feel a thing and I know where to take them afterwards. Somewhere they'll never be found."

Laura looked down the road at Dirk. He was still

coming, zig-zagging his way towards the van like a drunk with no destination. The head bouncing off his leg.

"I'll say this for the bastard," Roz said, watching him with cold eyes. "He's persistent. There's still something inside his scrambled brain, fighting for his kids. That's good. He's got hope. That's something else we can take away from him."

Laura could hear Dirk yelling behind the gag. Sounded like someone drowning in the distance, crying out for help.

"I've had enough."

Heart pounding, she walked towards the van. Reached for the back door. That's when Roz grabbed her by the wrist. Roz tugged on Laura's arm like it was a piece of rope in a tug of war contest. The force sent Laura backwards at speed. Away from the van. She tripped over her feet. Landed hard on the road, the rough surface scraping a chunk of skin off her back.

She cried out in pain.

The Remington slipped out of her grasp.

"What the fuck?"

"I'm sorry sweetie," Roz said, standing at the double doors. "But like I said. The sun's coming up and we don't have time for this. I'll take over, shall I?"

"No!"

Laura jumped back to her feet. She had to get to the rifle, but as soon as she was up, Roz charged straight at her, lashing out with the butt of the Remington. It struck Laura on top of the head. Bright lights flashed. White dots. Black dots. Red dots. She went sideways, then toppled over. But there was a voice screaming inside her head. Telling her she couldn't stay down.

"Are you fucking insane?" she yelled. "Are you going to kill me too?"

By now, the kids were screaming inside the van. Their gags barely suppressing the noise.

Roz turned to Laura. A disappointed look on her face. "See what you've done? You scared them. I was going to bring them out, turn them around and bang. They wouldn't have known what hit them."

She grabbed the handle, pulling the door open. Once again, sobs and screams gushed out from inside the Grand California.

There was no talking to Roz. Laura understood that now. No way of reaching her. Those people inside the van would die, whether Roz waited for Dirk to show up and witness it or not.

Laura tried to get up. Her body was sluggish, limbs all spongy, beaten up and exhausted. She looked to her right.

The rifle. She could almost reach it.

"Roz," she begged. "Stop."

Roz didn't even turn around. "Don't worry, hon. I'm a perfect shot, remember?"

Laura knew one thing for sure. Roz wasn't bluffing. Roz never bluffed. With time running out for Isla and Joe, she reached for the Remington. Felt like she was moving in slow motion. Like someone was holding her back. Her fingertips crawled forwards, inches from the barrel. Sweat gushed down her face. Heart pounding.

"Roz. Please."

But Roz wasn't listening. She was still facing the children. Singing the chorus of 'Daydream Believer' as she took a step back and raised the rifle.

35

DIRK

Dirk emerged through the woods, trampling over a strip of purple heather. He hurried onto the gravel. Onto the road. Pedalling on legs that had nothing left. He focused on the headlights up ahead, trying to speak behind the gag.

"I'm coming."

Uhmm cammin.

His skin and clothes were soaked with sweat. At least Diana's head wasn't talking anymore. He had to get it off before the kids saw it, but he was still handcuffed. What could he do? Taking it off meant looking her in the eyes. No, no, no.

One thing at a time.

The priority was rescuing Isla and Joe, even if the head was still there.

He shuffled forwards, limping towards the van. Lungs screaming for oxygen. He saw a flurry of movement in the yellowy-orange fog of light that surrounded the Grand California. Looked like a struggle at the back doors. Dirk strained his eyes. Two women. The big one pushing the little one onto the road.

Hallelujah, the bitches were fighting amongst themselves. Why? What were they disagreeing about? Were the kids still alive?

He stopped.

The sound of a single gunshot turned his blood cold.

Dirk wanted to run back into the woods. Away from the guns. But he knew the head would start talking to him again, calling him all sorts of names. He had to go forward. Even if it meant death.

With the last of his strength, he struggled along the edge of the road. Labouring up the incline. *Uhmm cammin!* Wincing at the stinging sensation in his hands and feet. Legs heavy, like two pillars of lead.

Uhmm cammin! Uhmm cammin!

36

Laura sat on the road, her body shaking. There was a blanket of silence around Camore Wood, so intense it felt like the world had stopped.

She hadn't moved since squeezing the trigger.

The Remington in her hands was still pointing at the van. She could still see it in her mind's eye – the bullet exploding in Roz's back. Or was it the shoulder she hit? God knows. It was already a blur. Something she had to convince herself had happened. Laura had been so terrified she was surprised she'd hit anything. She shot her friend. But she *had* to do it. There'd been no reasoning with Roz in the end.

Roz didn't scream. Didn't yell. Didn't cry out in pain. She'd crashed to the ground with a vicious thud, but she wasn't dead. All that blood leaking out of her, its trail reddish-black in the gloomy fog of the Highland dawn. She didn't look at Laura. Didn't speak. After managing to flip on to her stomach, she'd crawled away on all fours, making her way to the other side of the road. Bleeding. Gasping for air. It was the agonising journey of a wounded animal disappearing into the woods.

Laura felt helpless. It was her fault.

All of it.

She was the one who called Roz at Fyrish Monument. Told her all about Dirk this morning, opening up old wounds. Roz didn't need to hear any of it. She had her own demons to slay and something about Dirk and what he did to Laura must have started the wheels turning. She was quick to arrive at Fyrish. And, with the duffel bag over her shoulder, it was clear she was ready for a long night. Ready to do anything to hurt him, which meant hurting his family. Innocent people.

Fuck.

Why did Laura have to see Dirk at Skiach? Why did she have to look over at that table, then get up and chase after him? Why did she have to get in his car five years ago? She could have gone out with the other girls that night, ventured on to a nightclub, or shared an Uber or a taxi with someone else. Yet she'd gone with Budz, ending up with Dirk de Vries behind the wheel, the unhinged driver who was losing his family.

Fuck. Fuck. Fuck.

Laura struggled back to her feet. Every step caused her to wince. Her hands were badly scraped. Felt like she'd grabbed a scalding kettle. The weight of an elephant was on her back. She hobbled forward, taking an exaggerated step over the blood on the road, approaching the back doors of the van.

She stared at them. Tied up on the bed, as they'd been for hours. Tears streaming down their faces. Eyes that looked straight at her. No shying away. Begging for mercy. Their gagged cries sounded painful, like choking. One last scream before dawn. They must have thought that Laura had come to finish them off. Looking down, she realised she still had the rifle in hand.

A glance to the right. A long trail of blood. No sign of Roz.

Laura had to decide what to do next. She could hear those scraping footsteps on the road. Closer. Louder. Dirk was coming.

37

Dirk pulled at the peeling corner of tape on his mouth. He ripped it off in one go, wincing at the sudden explosion of pain.

"Fuuuuuuuck!"

Damn it, he *could* reach it. He could've leaned over and pulled the tape off his mouth at any time. The cuffs weren't stopping him – it was his mind. The acid. Fucking acid had scrambled his mind. Making him run in and out of the woods, going back to the road, to the headlights, and the two crazies who kept dragging him back in. But all that was over. He was thinking straight now.

"I'm coming!"

He ran towards the van. The red-golden dawn was overwhelming and it energised Dirk, who felt like he was waking up from the worst nightmare he'd ever had, waking up to a morning that he thought he'd never see.

Bump.

Diana was still there. Still with him. What was he supposed to tell the kids? The true horror of what had happened to his wife would only sink in when he stopped.

Dirk had to reach them. Isla. Joe. They were the only family he had left. His legs worked overtime, wringing out the last of his energy supplies. His chest was tight, legs full of cement.

"I'm coming," he said again, his voice a wheezy retch.

He focused on the headlights. Saw the blue-haired monster first. Running around to the side of the campervan, opening up the driver's side door.

"Hey! What did you do to my children?"

Dirk's voice sounded like someone being strangled. The monster paid no attention to him. She was in the van now. Door slammed shut. Her eyes locked on the road ahead.

He tried speeding up, but it was no use. The van roared and took off, its sudden acceleration causing Dirk to trip over his feet. He went down hard on a bed of dirt and gravel, his knees and elbows taking the worst of it.

"Stop!"

Diana's hair brushed off the tip of his elbow. Dirk gasped, like his insides had morphed to ice. Still, he wouldn't look. *Couldn't* look. The dead haziness of her eyes would haunt him forever. Not those eyes. The ones he loved. The ones that loved him back five years ago. He wanted to remember the way Diana's eyes lit up when she talked about her dreams, about circling the NC500 with her family. That was his wife. Not this this *thing* tied to his leg. That was meat.

He buried his face in his hands. The cuffs rattled.

"I'm sorry."

Words. Weak words.

Dirk pushed himself back to his feet. He was all cuts and scrapes. Felt like someone with a grudge was sawing his head in half. He wheezed as he staggered up the road. Further down the track, he saw the Grand California jerk in advance of a left turn. The engine howling. It tore through the turn and its taillights disappeared.

The woods were silent.

Dirk spun around at the sound of footsteps.

"Dad!"

He gasped as Isla ran down the track towards him. A manic sprint, kicking up clouds of dirt. Long hair flowing behind her. Arms open wide. She slammed into Dirk, wrapping her arms around his waist. Squeezing him. Dirk collapsed into his stepdaughter's embrace. Tears pouring down his cheeks.

"Dad."

"Isla."

Somehow, she was able to hold him up.

The head, he thought. *She's pressing against her mother's head and hasn't noticed.*

There was a thumping sound on the road. He looked beyond Isla's shoulder. Saw something else. Something that made Dirk wonder if he was dreaming or perhaps he was dead or dying in the woods. Staring at the light at the end of the tunnel. Waiting for his heart to stop beating.

Diana was running towards him.

She had Joe by the hand. They were coming downhill, almost as fast as Isla had. She was alive. She was intact, head and neck still joined together.

Dirk staggered backwards, letting go of Isla. He reached for his wife, not daring to trust his eyes.

"It's not p-p-possible."

He was about to look at the thing on his leg. There was no time before Diana and Joe were on him. Wrapping their arms around him and, along with Isla, forming a group hug. Dirk cried. He bawled, emptying the tank. His heart pounded. It felt like he was being strangled but he didn't care. The family were back together. They all cried, dropping to their knees, kissing each other, crying some more and thanking whatever god had showed them mercy.

After about a minute, Dirk came up for air. He looked towards the road, to where the Grand California had been parked minutes earlier. Saw a dark puddle on the track. At first, he thought it was oil. Then he realised it was blood. A long trail of blood that led to the other side of the road.

He battled to get the words out. "What happened?"

It was Joe who answered. "She shot her."

Dirk frowned. "Who shot who?"

Diana took over from Joe. She placed a hand over her chest, pressing it down, as if to keep her heart from leaping out. Her words were crammed in between frantic gulps of air. "The woman...with...the blue hair. She...shot the big one."

"Why?"

"Don't know...how it started. There was a fight. It got ugly. I think the one with blue hair...was trying to help us."

"Is the big one dead?" Dirk asked.

Diana pointed to the trees across the road. "She crawled over that way. I couldn't see much after that. She must have...disappeared into the forest. God knows if she's still alive. After that, the other one...she just let us go and drove off. We saw you running up the–"

Diana squinted. She took a step back. Pointed at Dirk's leg.

"What the hell is *that*?"

Dirk did what he'd been avoiding for hours. He looked down. *Shit*, he thought. *Oh shit*. It was a fake head. Of course it was. A mannequin's head with black, stringy hair and a bloody severed neck. Fake. So obviously fake. And yet, so convincing in the dark. Even more convincing because Dirk had refused to look at it. One look would have cleared everything up. Told him that Diana wasn't dead. Damn thing. It looked like a horror movie prop or a grisly Halloween decoration.

He looked at Diana. Looked at the head. Didn't want to tell her but couldn't stop himself.

"I thought it was you."

"What?"

Diana grabbed it by the hair, snapping the string that held it to Dirk's leg. There was a popping noise. She held the head aloft, stared at it. A look of disgust on her face. Then, she tossed it onto the side of the road.

"You thought *that* was me?"

Dirk nodded. "It was dark...they gave me something... wasn't thinking straight."

Diana put her arms around her children. She shivered. Pulled them close while looking down the road, wary of the Grand California coming back. Or maybe it was the giant she was scared of. It was still too early to believe that the nightmare was over.

"We need to go," she said. "We need help."

The four of them started walking down the track, sticking to the edges where the woods began. Kicking up gravel. Legs stiff. Not much talk. There was a lot of looking over their shoulders every minute or so. Hoping that a car would come along or that they'd find a road, a house or something that resembled salvation.

Thank God for the sun coming up.

Isla and Joe walked shoulder to shoulder at the front. Dirk and Diana were a few paces behind them. Holding hands.

Dirk could hear Isla asking Joe questions about his guitar. Asking about what sort of music he'd play when he

got it. What make of guitar he'd get. Fender? Gibson? It kept
Joe's mind occupied while they walked. For his part, Dirk
felt drained. Like he'd been turned inside out. He feared the
nightmares that would come over the following days.

He felt Diana let go of his hand.

"Dirk?"

"Uh-huh?"

There was a cold emptiness where her hand had been.
He tried to pull her back and she resisted. She was looking
at the kids. Slowing down, as if to let them get a little further
ahead. Finally, she looked at him. A hardness forming in her
eyes. One that left Dirk uneasy.

"Are you okay?" he asked.

Silence.

"Diana? What is it?"

"Dirk. Is there something you want to tell me?"

He felt his skin burning. "W-w-what do you mean?"

"You're stuttering," she said. "You never stutter with me."

Dirk tried to laugh it off. It came out all wrong. Sounded
like he was having a stroke. "It's been a rough night. What's
going on here?"

Diana lowered her voice. "When that woman tied us up
last night, she asked if I knew who I was married to. If I
really knew. The way she said it–"

Dirk felt a pinch of fear. "She's a madwoman. You can't
listen to–"

"It was you," she said. "Wasn't it?"

Dirk felt like he'd been hit by a bolt of lightning. "W-w-
what?"

"This thing that happened to us, it wasn't just a random
attack. It didn't come out of nowhere. It had something to do
with you. Something you've done."

He couldn't speak. Couldn't move. Couldn't do anything

except look at her. There was no point in lying – the truth was right there in his eyes and he knew it. A confession, spilling out without words.

Diana's eyes were cold. All the love gone in that moment, slipping away like grains of sand through fingers. She walked away from him. Caught up with her children and put her arms around their shoulders, holding on tight. Shielding them. From who? From Dirk?

Dirk watched them go, unable to follow.

The sun was almost up over Camore Wood. But Dirk, feeling that old familiar emptiness rising up inside, realised that he wasn't out of danger.

Far from it.

He'd just lost another family.

38

LAURA

Sometimes, they came early. Some of them drove all night to get to Roz's farmhouse. True crime junkies. They'd knock on the door and more often than not, Roz would answer with the rifle in hand. That tended to get the point across without having to speak to these bloodsuckers.

Laura hit the brakes as the Grand California crawled up the driveway.

There was already a car parked outside the house. She could see two people, a man and a woman, walking around the front of the house. Peering into the living room window. Taking photos.

Today, there'd be no answer. No Roz telling them to fuck off or threatening to shoot their tyres if they didn't mind their own business.

Laura brought the van to a stop. She looked to the surrounding fields. Miles and miles of empty, mostly over-grown grass that stretched all the way to the tortoise-shell hills in the distance. Laura had tried calling Roz's mobile.

No answer. She imagined Roz somewhere out there on all fours, crawling through the tall grass towards the farmhouse. Her chalk-white face staring ahead, hands covered in blood.

She parked beside the Range Rover. Metallic red, its bonnet gleaming under the morning sun. The dark tourists came to Roz's house in all forms of transport. Cars, bikes, motorcycles. They got the train to Alness, then walked or hitchhiked the rest of the way. Once, a busload of true crime fanatics from Japan who were on a UK tour, pulled up outside the house and started taking photos. Roz told Laura that the bastards knocked on her door for an hour. Even tried the door handle. Roz hid under the bed.

The two vampires didn't seem fazed by Laura's arrival. They were busy with their phones, taking photographs, recording audio notes. The man had a small video camera hanging around his neck.

All these people, whether they were from Japan, Argentina, the States, Germany, and all the other places, were fascinated by the documentaries they'd seen. The podcasts they'd heard. Books they'd read. Some were writing books of their own. Others were making TV shows. It was easy to find the house, which was barely a minute's drive off the A9. A grisly stop on the NC500. One that wasn't mentioned in the guide books.

Laura got out the van. She walked past a rusty wheelbarrow on the grass, a shovel and a bunch of other worn-out tools.

There was a pleasant breeze drifting in from the north. The sky, clear except for the long condensation trail left by a passing aircraft.

"Good morning."

The man waved at Laura. The woman did likewise as

they approached the driveway from the opposite end of the house.

Laura's head was groggy from lack of sleep. That and the rest of it. There was a faint ringing in her right ear that wouldn't quit.

"Morning. You do know this is private property, don't you?"

"We knocked on the front door," the man said, his smile fizzling out. He sounded French. Mid-thirties. Arab-looking, thick arched eyebrows. Dark hair tied back into a ponytail. "Nobody was home. So–"

Laura pulled at the neck of her t-shirt. One minute she was cold, the next burning hot. "So you started taking pictures anyway?"

"Umm–"

The woman came to her companion's rescue. She was every bit as French. Tall, blonde, and dressed in a sleek shirt and trouser combo that made her look like a roving reporter from a Superman comic. Definitely a city girl.

"No harm done, right?

"Are *you* a tourist?" the man asked Laura. "Podcaster? Filmmaker?"

"I live nearby. She's a friend of mine."

They told her their names. Marie and Vincent. Proceeded to explain what they were doing. Recording a podcast for their 'award-winning' show. Blah-blah. Laura barely listened to a word of it. She glanced over Marie's perfect shoulders. Searching for movement on the hillside. All Laura could think about was that long smear of blood on the single-track road. The sight of Roz, crawling towards the woods. No eye contact. No words. Nothing. Like she'd accepted it.

Those children would be dead if she hadn't squeezed the trigger.

That's what Laura was hanging on to.

"I assume you know the history?" Marie said. She held up both hands. "Of course you do if you're local."

Vincent shrugged. "Maybe not. Maybe Roz doesn't talk about it."

"I know it," Laura said. "Everyone around here knows it."

Vincent's eyes narrowed in concentration. He was facing the house again. Looked like he was lining up another shot.

"Who doesn't know the story of Roz Clarke?" he said, as if talking to himself. "Not an easy story to forget, *oui*? A local artist, attacked in this very house on Christmas Eve by her ex-husband. The same ex-husband who, ten years earlier, killed their daughter in London and tried to make it look like an accident."

Marie's smile faded as she surveyed the garden. The withered grass. Vacant flower beds spilling over with weeds. The broken-down tools. For the first time since Laura's arrival, she looked uncomfortable. Realising perhaps, what most people around these parts had known for years. That Roz's house was more than just a dark tourist spot.

"He went to prison," Vincent said, continuing the story, "and got out early for good behaviour. There's no justice in the world, no?"

Laura shook her head. "None."

Vincent wagged his finger in the air. "Then what does he do? He starts looking for her. He tracks Roz down here where she's started a new life, trying to move on from the London tragedy. But that's not what he wants. He wants to punish her for testifying against him in court. Instead of going along with the 'accident theory'."

He looked at Laura. His eyes blazing with excitement.

"I can't imagine what it was like for her that night. When she answered the door and saw–"

"He made a mistake," Laura said. "It was the last mistake he ever made. Coming here. Thinking he was just going to pick up where they left off. But Roz wasn't the same submissive wife he'd known in London. Not even close. Ten years is a long time."

Marie nodded. "And she'd learned how to use a gun."

"Even more important," Laura said, "she'd become the sort of person willing to use one. When it mattered most."

"It was self-defence," Vincent said, browsing through some of the photos he'd already taken that morning. "Perfectly justified. And the law agreed."

Laura sighed. "It was never enough. Not for Roz."

"What do you mean?" Marie asked.

"It was never enough to make up for losing her daughter. In the end, she could only kill that bastard once."

Marie was staring at the hills. She seemed in awe of the rugged beauty of this place. "And to think, he was such a white-collar guy, huh? A big-name entrepreneur. A celebrity, loved by all."

Laura nodded. "A nice family man."

"Right."

Vincent finally shoved his phone into his pocket. He took a step back, surveying the farmhouse. The crumbling wooden exterior, the foliage intruding across its walls, and the square gaps where the windows used to be.

"May we interview you?"

"What?"

"We could buy you breakfast. Sit down. Just an hour, if you don't mind?"

Laura didn't like the way Vincent was looking at her. Like a thing. Like something to be squeezed.

"I have to go."

"No, I'm sorry."

She looked at the house one last time. Laura knew she was going to have to live with pulling Roz into the Dirk situation yesterday. She'd opened up the darkness in Roz and in the end, it was too much. Still, she had to believe that Roz was still alive. Still out there, fighting to make it home.

The French podcasters called out to her as she walked away. But Laura didn't turn around. She'd said too much as it was. She got back into the campervan and started the engine. Turned the Grand California around, rolled it down the driveway and steered through the open gate back onto the road.

Laura drove south for about a mile, eyes still roaming the landscape.

She pulled into a lay-by. The sort of lay-by she'd spent so much time in over the past five years, selling handmade jewellery to tourists. With the engine still ticking, Laura checked her phone. Two fresh missed calls from yesterday.

She stared through the windscreen at the empty road. No traffic. No birds singing. The world had never been so quiet.

She put the phone to her ear. Heard it ringing.

A click.

Her mother's voice, frantic with excitement.

"Laura. Oh my God! Is that you darling?"

"It's me."

Laura heard her dad's voice in the background. He sounded every bit as excited as her mother. She'd never heard him so giddy in all her life.

"Is it her? Is it Laura?"

Her mother's voice was back in her ear. Fighting back the tears. "Oh darling, is that really you? We've missed you so much. We're sorry. We're so sorry that...that we weren't there for you. That we didn't believe in you. Where are you? Where are you now, sweetheart?"

Laura couldn't speak. A quick glance at the dashboard. There was plenty of fuel in the tank to get started.

Her mother's shrill voice in her ear pulled her back.

"Where are you, Laura? What are you doing now?"

Laura's foot touched the accelerator. The Grand California shuddered, then pulled out of the lay-by and made its way back onto the road.

A last glance at the hills. Then, finally, she found the words.

"I'm coming home."

THE END

OTHER THRILLER/SUSPENSE BOOKS
BY MARK GILLESPIE

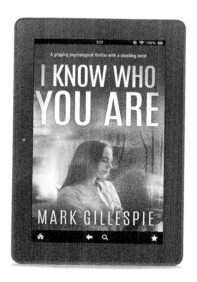

Two lives connected by tragedy. Destined to collide. And at the end, one mind-blowing secret will be revealed...

I Know Who You Are - start reading today!

Lisa Granger did the unthinkable. She committed a shocking act of betrayal that no one would ever believe.

One year later, there's a price to pay.

And the cost is everything...

Make It Up To Me

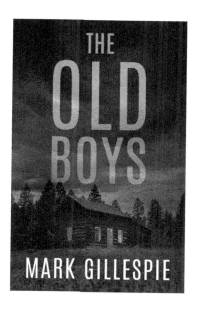

Three men are kidnapped on the eve of their high school reunion and wake up trapped inside a remote cabin in the Scottish Highlands.

What comes next is the discovery that one of them is a killer.

The Old Boys

MARK GILLESPIE
I'LL BE
NEXT TO
VANISH

Horrifying revelations, buried for years, are about to come to light. Greed, paranoia, kidnapping and murder.

And it's all connected to the shocking truth about Ryker Marshall's disappearance.

I'll Be Next To Vanish

POST APOCALYPTIC/DYSTOPIAN TITLES BY MARK GILLESPIE

After the End Trilogy

The Exterminators Trilogy

Dystopiaville

The Butch Nolan Trilogy

Mark Gillespie's author website
   www.markgillespieauthor.com

Mark Gillespie on Facebook
   www.facebook.com/markgillespieswritingstuff

Mark Gillespie on Twitter
   www.twitter.com/MarkG_Author

Mark Gillespie on Bookbub
   https://www.bookbub.com/profile/mark-gillespie

Printed in Great Britain
by Amazon

34799916R10158